The Windmill of Love

Valeria could not raise her eyes to meet the *Duc*'s.

Then she heard him say in his deep voice:

"I am delighted to meet you, Lady Valeria, and to welcome you to my Château."

He spoke in English in a calm, cold ~~~~ which struck her as ~

She looked up at l

As she did so, he t

his relatives.

It seemed incredib

her!

A Camfield Novel of Love
by Barbara Cartland

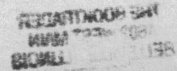

Camfield Place,
Hatfield
Hertfordshire,
England

Dearest Reader,

Camfield Novels of Love mark a very exciting era of my books with Jove. They have already published nearly two hundred of my titles since they became my first publisher in America, and now all my original paperback romances in the future will be published exclusively by them.

As you already know, Camfield Place in Hertfordshire is my home, which originally existed in 1275, but was rebuilt in 1867 by the grandfather of Beatrix Potter.

It was here in this lovely house, with the best view in the county, that she wrote *The Tale of Peter Rabbit*. Mr. McGregor's garden is exactly as she described it. The door in the wall that the fat little rabbit could not squeeze underneath and the goldfish pool where the white cat sat twitching its tail are still there.

I had Camfield Place blessed when I came here in 1950 and was so happy with my husband until he died, and now with my children and grandchildren, that I know the atmosphere is filled with love and we have all been very lucky.

It is easy here to write of love and I know you will enjoy the Camfield Novels of Love. Their plots are definitely exciting and the covers very romantic. They come to you, like all my books, with love.

Bless you,

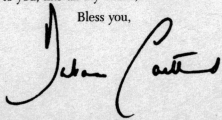

CAMFIELD NOVELS OF LOVE

by Barbara Cartland

A NEW CAMFIELD NOVEL OF LOVE BY

BARBARA CARTLAND

The Windmill of Love

JOVE BOOKS, NEW YORK

THE WINDMILL OF LOVE

A Jove Book / published by arrangement with
the author

PRINTING HISTORY
Jove edition / March 1992

ISBN: 0-515-10811-1

Jove Books are published by The Berkley Publishing Group,
200 Madison Avenue, New York, New York 10016.
The name "JOVE" and the "J" logo
are trademarks belonging to Jove Publications, Inc.

PRINTED IN THE UNITED STATES OF AMERICA

10 9 8 7 6 5 4 3 2 1

Author's Note

A Spanish noblewoman discovered the charm of Biarritz when it was still a small, unimportant village.

In 1838 the Countess de Montijo and her daughter Eugénie began going there each year.

When Eugénie became the Empress of France she persuaded Napoleon III to visit the Basque Coast and build a residence for her called "The Villa Eugénie."

Biarritz became famous and at the beginning of this century was the favourite holiday resort of Edward VII.

On October 6th, 1889, in Paris, the *Moulin Rouge* opened its doors and made the *Can-Can* world-famous.

The *Can-Can* had been born during the Second Empire and was a variation of *le chahut*, which had been the delight of the working classes.

But at the *Moulin Rouge* it became the symbol of what was to be called "The Naughty Nineties."

A fleeting glimpse of perhaps two inches of bare flesh between stockings and frilly knickers played a vital part in spreading the myth of "Naughty Paris."

Apart from the dance, which was the most spectacular amusement in Paris, the programme contained a dancer known as *La Goulue,* who was highly erotic.

She was so unusual and fantastic that the Journalists and Chroniclers of Paris in the 1890s devoted a great many pages to a description of her.

One describes her as having:

> . . . a nose with quivering, impatient nostrils, a nose of one sniffing after love, nostrils dilating with the male odour of chestnut trees and the enervating bouquet of brandy glasses.

She was a part of the great period when for people throughout the world the *Moulin Rouge* became the synonym for Montmartre and Paris. In fact, it was another word for "Pleasure."

chapter one

1891

THE Earl of Netherton-Strangeways drummed his fingers on the desk as he waited.

He was a good-looking man of great importance at Court as well as having a position among the aristocrats that was second to none.

The Netherton family had played its part all through history.

The 7th Earl had every intention of continuing the tradition.

He thought with a sense of irritation that his son the Viscount Strang was feckless.

He was too intent upon enjoying himself rather than attending to his duties.

At the same time, the Earl was sensible enough to accept that "boys will be boys" and that he should not expect too much from his attractive son.

On the other hand, his daughter Valeria was, he thought, extremely intelligent besides being very beautiful.

This was not surprising considering that her Mother had been acclaimed as one of the greatest beauties in London.

The Countess had a fascination which, the Earl was obliged to admit, was due to her French ancestry.

She had been half French because her Father, the Marquess of Melchester, had married the daughter of the *Duc* de Chamois.

Even to think of his wife, who had died two years earlier, brought sadness to the Earl's eyes.

He had married first into a family whose ancestry equalled his own.

It had been an arranged marriage which, like so many others, had failed both the bride and the bridegroom.

Although he preferred not to admit it, it had been a relief when, having produced a son and heir, his wife died.

It was less than two years later that the Earl remarried, this time for love.

He had been completely bowled over the first time he saw the face of Lady Yvonne Chester at a Ball which had taken place at Windsor Castle.

He fell very much in love.

He was also frantic lest he should lose the one woman he really wanted in his life.

They had been married in what the gossips referred to as "indecent haste."

They were blissfully happy from the moment they met.

Their only sadness was that Yvonne had been able to produce just one child—their daughter Valeria.

However, the Earl was thinking now, Valeria

had more than made up for any other children they might have had.

She was beautiful, a good rider, and she had a charisma which, like her Mother, attracted everybody to her.

The door opened and Valeria came into the room.

She seemed to bring the sunshine with her.

She said as she shut the door:

"Forgive me, Papa, if I have kept you waiting, but I was in the stables and they did not find me for some time!"

"I might have guessed that was where you would be," the Earl said, "and I suppose you are going to tell me that Crusader has jumped even higher than he did yesterday!"

This was a family joke, and Valeria laughed before she said:

"The jumps will have to be raised at least six inches!"

"Nonsense!" the Earl replied. "They are quite high enough already. Now, sit down, Valeria, I want to talk to you."

There was a serious note in her Father's voice which made Valeria look at him sharply.

"What is wrong, Papa?" she enquired.

"There is nothing wrong," the Earl answered, "but I have been thinking seriously about your future."

Valeria stiffened.

She had a presentiment that her Father would be speaking to her sooner or later about marriage.

She had known it was in his mind.

She had a habit of reading the thoughts of those she loved.

She had prayed to herself that she was mistaken.

Now she knew her prayers had not been answered.

"You are aware," the Earl began somewhat pompously, "that now that you have been presented at Court and the Season is nearly over, we should be thinking about your marriage."

Valeria stiffened, but she did not speak, and the Earl went on:

"I have given it a great deal of thought, and yesterday when I was in London I went to see your Grandmother."

Valeria laughed, and it was a very pretty sound.

She was devoted to her Grandmother, the Dowager Duchess of Melchester.

She knew that because she loved her she would not let her Father insist on her marrying somebody she disliked, or with whom she had no affinity.

Quickly, as if she anticipated what her Father was about to tell her, Valeria said:

"You remember, Papa, Mama always used to say that because you and she were so happy together, you would *never* make me marry somebody I did not love."

"I have not forgotten that," the Earl agreed, "but you have not told me of anyone to whom you have lost your heart."

Valeria smiled.

"I can assure you in all sincerity that there is no one! I have received proposals of marriage that I could not avoid, as well as a number of tentative advances which I have 'nipped in the bud.'"

The Earl laughed as if he could not help it.

"I am sure you did that very competently."

"I hope so," Valeria said. "I hate to hurt anyone, and it must be very humiliating for a man to lay his heart at a woman's feet only to have it trampled on."

"I think I know most of your suitors," the Earl said, "and I can only say that I disapprove of all of them!"

"I thought you would." Valeria smiled.

There was a silence until the Earl said:

"What your Grandmother has suggested, and of course I agree, is that you and I should go to France and be the guests of the *Duc* de Laparde."

Valeria was surprised and exclaimed:

"Grandmama has spoken of the *Duc* many times, but I never thought . . . I never . . . imagined that she was . . . thinking of . . . me as his *Duchesse*."

"I expect you already know," the Earl replied, "that the *Duc* was married when he was very young to a bride who was considered a suitable match by both his parents and hers."

Valeria nodded, and the Earl went on:

"Unfortunately the *Duc*'s parents discovered too late that there was a streak of insanity in the girl's family."

He paused a moment before continuing:

"As soon as they were married it appeared in a most unpleasant manner which both bewildered and disgusted her Bridegroom."

"It must have been a tragedy for him," Valeria said quietly.

"It was," the Earl agreed. "Finally the girl was taken into a Private Nursing-Home, where not even her closest relatives were allowed to visit her."

He was silent. Then he continued:

"As you have just said, it was a tragedy for a young man, who was only about twenty-two at the time. No one blamed him therefore when he consoled himself in Paris as well as in other amusing places in Europe."

"Grandmama told me that eventually his wife died."

"After two or three years, I believe," the Earl agreed, "and it was hardly surprising when Claudius Laparde declared that never again would he marry."

"I remember Grandmama telling me how upset his family were," Valeria said, "but one can understand his feelings."

"Of course, of course!" the Earl agreed. "But the *Duc* is now over thirty and your Grandmother has suggested that you and I invite ourselves to stay for a week or so at his Château, to see if you can change the *Duc*'s mind."

Valeria stared at her Father.

"Do you seriously believe that is possible, Papa?" she asked.

"It could happen," her father answered, "and, like your Grandmother, my dearest child, it would give me great pleasure to see you as a *Duchesse*."

Valeria made a little gesture with her hands, then was silent.

Then, quite unexpectedly, she laughed.

Her Father looked at her in surprise and she explained:

"Forgive me, Papa, but the whole idea is so preposterous, and it is so like Grandmama, who lives in a Fairyland of her own making! Being French, she is very romantic while at the same time being very practical."

She laughed again.

"Of course she wants the *Duc* to marry. At the same time, she would not choose anyone who is not, like your daughter, blue-blooded and had a very considerable dowry to bring to her future husband."

The mocking way in which Valeria spoke made the Earl's eyes twinkle.

Then he too laughed.

"As an innocent young *débutante,* you are not supposed to know of such things!" he declared.

"I may be innocent, but not idiotic, Papa. When Grandmama was talking about the *Duc* in the past and not thinking of me as his future wife, she told me of his many *affaires de coeur* with beautiful, exciting women! She made him sound like a modern Casanova!"

The Earl frowned.

"Your Grandmother should be more discreet!"

Valeria laughed again.

"That is something she will never be, and it is one of her greatest charms! She always says the unexpected."

"At thirty the *Duc* should have 'sown his wild oats' and be ready to settle down," the Earl remarked.

"For a Frenchman, that is very unlikely," Valeria replied, "as Grandmama explained to me in one of her indiscreet conversations. A Frenchman will treat his wife in public with the utmost politeness and consideration while at the same time he has an alluring lady tucked in his *garçonnière.*"

The Earl brought the flat of his hand down so

7

hard on the desk that it made the ink-pot rattle.

"Your Grandmother has no right to tell you such things!" he said severely. "I shall speak to her about it!"

"It is too late, Papa, the damage is done!" Valeria replied. "And the answer to your proposition is, quite simply, 'No'!"

"Very well," her Father said, "we must try some other way, for, as your Grandmother rightly pointed out, there are no eligible bachelors amongst the English Dukes. She had the impression also from what you said to her that you found the average English suitor somewhat boring."

"That is certainly true," Valeria replied. "They talk a great deal about horses, but most of them have never bothered to find out how they are bred or even how they are trained."

The Earl's eyes were twinkling again.

"That is hardly of consequence when it comes to marriage!"

"It is, as far as I am concerned!" Valeria argued.

"In that case," the Earl said, "I should tell you that the *Duc* has had considerable success with his race-horses and is, I believe, considered to be one of the best amateur riders in France."

"I too have heard that," Valeria replied, "but I would hate, Papa, to be an 'also ran' to some attractive Courtesan with whom he spends his time in Paris."

She saw the frown between her Father's eyes and said quickly:

"If you had behaved like that, can you imagine how hurt and unhappy Mama would have been?"

"I know, I know!" the Earl agreed. "At the same

8

time, my dearest, we have to face facts. The happiness I found with your Mother is something that happens only once in a million times."

"But that is what I want for myself," Valeria said softly.

"And God knows, it is what I want for you," her father answered. "But we cannot materialise out of thin air a man who will capture your heart and your imagination, so what are we going to do?"

Valeria thought for a moment. Then she said:

"What I think we will do, Papa, which will make Grandmama happy, is to go to stay with the *Duc* as she suggests."

The Earl looked at his daughter in surprise as she went on:

"I have always longed to see the Pyrenees, and if we are bored at the Château, as doubtless we will be, perhaps we could go to stay at Biarritz."

"It is certainly an idea," the Earl agreed.

"Then I will go with you on one condition," Valeria said, "and that is if you will promise me—and you never break your promises, Papa—that you will not try to persuade me to marry the *Duc,* even if he should, which I very much doubt, wish to marry me."

"I made that promise to your Mother," the Earl said, "so there is no reason for me not to make the same promise to you. But I agree it would be amusing to see the *Duc*'s Château over which your Grandmother continually enthuses."

"Grandmama makes it sound like a mixture of Kublai Khan's Palace and the Garden of Eden," Valeria said. "I am very doubtful if any place could be so perfect, except for Paradise itself!"

The Earl laughed.

"Then we must go and find out and, as you say, it would be amusing to see Biarritz. Her Majesty was talking about the place only the other day and how much she enjoyed her visit there two years ago."

"We will have a great deal of fun, Papa, and when we return to England we will make a list of all the eligible bachelors of whom we both approve."

"You are saying that merely to placate me," the Earl complained. "At the same time, there must be a man somewhere in the world who can live up to your high standards!"

"My requirements are quite simple," Valeria replied. "I want to marry a man I love, and who loves me."

She paused before she added:

"And he must, Papa, be as good-looking, as kind, understanding, and at least half as intelligent as you are!"

The Earl held up his hands.

"Now you are flattering me, and you are doing it in that irresistible French manner of which your mother was a past-master!"

Valeria walked around the desk and, bending down, kissed her Father.

"I love you, Papa," she said, "and quite frankly I am so happy at home that I have no wish to go away and live in a strange house with a strange man, even if he is as grand as the Shah of Persia!"

"You know I want to keep you with me," the Earl replied. "At the same time, my darling, as your Grandmother pointed out, it is always wise for a beautiful woman to be married when she is young."

"What Grandmama was implying is that I might have an unfortunate love-affair with somebody I could not marry," Valeria answered. "Do not worry, Papa, the only person I am in love with at the moment is Crusader, and to be honest, I find him far more attractive than any man have yet met."

The Earl laughed, and, rising, put his arm around his daughter.

"It must be nearly luncheon time," he said, "and the best thing we can both do this afternoon is to go riding."

"I would love that, Papa, if you have nothing better to do," Valeria replied.

"Nothing could be better than to ride together," the Earl said as he smiled, "but before we go I will write a letter to the *Duc* suggesting we come and stay with him in a fortnight's time."

Valeria thought for a moment.

"That would be about right," she said. "All the best Balls will be over by then: and that reminds me—we are going to one this evening, or had you forgotten?"

"No, of course not," the Earl replied, "considering that we have promised to have thirty guests to dinner."

"I am looking forward to dancing with the windows open onto the garden. It is much more attractive than being cooped up in London when the weather is hot."

"Cooped up or not," the Earl remarked, "we have a number of engagements next week for which I want you to look your best."

Valeria gave him a sharp glance.

"Are you still match-making, Papa?" she asked.

"Oh, do stop it! If this miraculous man appears, he will doubtless drop down the chimney!"

She gave a little laugh before she went on:

"Alternatively, if that is what the gods decree, I will meet him when I am riding in Rotten Row, or find him sitting next to me at one of those long-drawn-out dinner-parties which, quite frankly, I find as boring as you do!"

"Who told you I find them boring?" her Father asked sharply.

"I do not need to be told," Valeria answered. "You *look* bored, and it is not surprising. You always have the oldest and dullest women on either side of you because they are the most important! I am sure you would rather have someone young and pretty, like me!"

The Earl laughed.

"Anyone as young and pretty as you would not want someone as old and dull as me to talk to!"

"Do not be too sure about that, Papa," Valeria replied. "As I love and admire you so much, I shall doubtless marry an octogenarian, or perhaps one of those Gentlemen-in-Waiting at Buckingham Palace who I was thinking only the other day must all be over eighty!"

The Earl laughed again.

When two minutes later he walked towards the Dining-Room with his daughter on his arm, he was thinking how like her Mother she was.

Everything she did and said seemed to sparkle, and it was impossible for anyone to be bored when they were in her company.

'I have to find her a husband who will learn to love and understand her,' he thought.

He knew it was going to be a difficult task.

In fact, because of Valeria's positive views, it was going to be very, very difficult.

* * *

Ten days later Valeria was upstairs in her bedroom at Strang House in Park Lane.

She was sorting out the gowns she intended to take with her to France.

She discarded those which were too worn after the Season and not elegant enough to be appreciated by the French.

In his reply to her father's letter the *Duc* had written enthusiastically.

He was looking forward to seeing the Earl, as he wished to discuss his race-horses with him and obtain his opinion on those he had recently acquired.

> *. . . and of course I shall be delighted for you to bring your daughter Lady Valeria with you.*

The letter was reassuring as far as Valeria was concerned.

It was clear the *Duc* did not realise why the visit had been proposed by the Dowager Duchess.

Her Grandmother, whom Valeria had gone to see when she was back in London, had assured her that she had never even hinted at the idea of marriage when she had written to the *Duc*.

"I write to him frequently," the Duchess said, "and of course I tell him about the success your Father has had on the Race-Course. After all, your Mother was the first cousin of the *Duc*'s father, and relationship in France counts for a great deal."

"You are quite certain, Grandmama, you did not suggest as you did to Papa that the *Duc* and I should be married?"

"Of course not," the Dowager Duchess replied, "and I assure you, my dear, that if Claudius thought he was being manoeuvred into a trap, he would be over the horizon long before you put in an appearance."

"I call that very sensible of him," Valeria remarked.

"There is nothing sensible about a man in his position without an heir," the Dowager Duchess said. "Think, dearest child, of that glorious Château, with the Pyrenees forming a background to it, of that big house in the Champs-Élysées and his horses—and, *Mon Dieu*—what horses they are!"

Valeria laughed.

"Now you are trying to tempt me, Grandmama, and I can only say quite firmly, 'Get thee behind me, Satan!' "

The Dowager Duchess, who was still beautiful at nearly eighty, threw up her hands in despair.

"You are impossible—quite impossible!" she complained. "Who are you waiting for? The King of Siam or the Angel Gabriel?"

"I think the Archangel Michael would be more appropriate," Valeria replied, "but as he is not available, I shall just have to go on looking."

Her Grandmother sighed.

"You know, *ma Petite*, I want your happiness, and no woman, I promise you, can be happy if she becomes an 'Old Maid.' "

"There is plenty of time before I reach that stage,"

Valeria said, "and I would rather be an 'Old Maid' than be bored or made miserable by a man with whom I had nothing in common."

The Dowager Duchess gave a little cry of horror.

"You are being blind when you are so beautiful! My dear child, what are women for, except to amuse and capture a man?"

"But only if they are worth capturing," Valeria said, "and as I told Papa, I find Crusader so much more attractive than any of them!"

"Horses—always horses!" the Dowager Duchess exclaimed in frustration. "But there at least you and Claudius would have something to talk about in the long winter evenings."

"Only if he was there, Grandmama! And you will remember that it was you who told me of the attractions of Paris about which all nicely brought up young girls are completely ignorant."

"*Tiens!* It is my tongue—my unfortunate tongue!" the Dowager Duchess said despairingly. "I say too much, then I regret it!"

Valeria laughed and kissed her Grandmother.

"You can never talk too much for me," she said, "and I love your stories of all the people you knew when you were young. I have also enjoyed everything you have told me about the dashing *Duc* who, Château or no Château, will always be off to 'Pastures new.' "

The Dowager Duchess again held up her hands in horror.

As she left the house, Valeria was smiling.

'Forewarned is forearmed!' she told herself. 'And at least I shall not be deceived by anything the *Duc* says. Nor will I be so foolish as to fall in love with him, as Grandmama hopes.'

At the same time, she was sure he would be very critical and dismiss her as an unfledged *jeune fille*.

It was the Dowager Duchess who had said to Valeria some time ago when they were talking about him:

"I wish Claudius could find a girl amongst the French aristocratic families who would make him the sort of wife he should have."

That was before it had struck the Dowager Duchess that the difficult and raffish Claudius might be linked with her.

"There must be plenty of *jeunes filles* in France!" Valeria had said.

"That is undoubtedly so," her Grandmother had replied, "but it is doubtful if Claudius has ever spoken to one. No, the women he enjoys are beautiful, sophisticated, exotic, and inevitably, of course, married!"

She was talking in her usual frank manner, but in French.

It made what she said sound less blunt than it would have in English.

Valeria had listened to her Grandmother wide-eyed as she always did.

She found everything she said fascinating, and certainly far more interesting than any of her English relatives.

She always felt that secretly they resented the happiness her father had found with a woman who was half-French.

It had been impossible for anyone not to have

seen the difference between them and the Countess.

Every word she spoke sparkled, and her beauty had an inner radiance.

She also had that indefinable *chic* which always distinguishes the French from any other nationality.

Even when she was quite small Valeria used to think how dull her English relatives looked when she compared them to her Mother.

The moment Yvonne entered a room the tempo seemed to rise.

People who had been sitting looking rather bored quickly became animated.

Valeria could quite understand why her Father's eyes continually rested on her Mother's glowing face.

When they spoke to each other their love seemed to vibrate from them as if it were a light which came from their hearts.

'That is how I want to feel, and how I want the man I marry to feel about me,' she told herself as soon as she could read romantic stories and identify herself with the heroine.

Valeria therefore wanted a man who stood out from other men—a Knight in Shining Armour, a Hero, a Leader!

At the same time, he would have ideals which she found, as she grew up, had either been forgotten by most men, or else they had never had them.

Now, as she took down yet another gown from the wardrobe, she told herself that going to France with her Father would at least be an adventure.

She would not confess even to herself that she had

been disappointed at her first Season in London.

Perhaps she had expected too much, but somehow each Ball she had attended had seemed to be a repetition of the last.

At dinner-parties the men seated on each side of her were boring.

Afterwards she could not remember one interesting thing she had learned from any of her partners.

She certainly never lacked for them.

Yet, she wondered cynically, would the overwhelming compliments she received have been fulsome had she not been her Father's daughter with a fortune of her own?

"I am enjoying myself—of course I am enjoying myself," she would try to say convincingly several times a day.

But if the truth was known, she would have been happier if she could have been riding in the country with Crusader as her only companion.

"Marry me, please, marry me!" one of her partners begged at the last Ball of the Season she had attended. "I love you, Valeria, you know I love you, and I will make you happy."

"I am sorry, Simon," she replied gently. "But while I like you very much, when I marry, I want to be in love."

"I will make you fall in love with me!"

Valeria had shaken her head.

"It is not as easy as that! Love is either there or it is not, and if it is not, there is nothing one can do about it."

"Let me kiss you," he said fiercely. "If I cannot convince you with words, I will convince you with kisses!"

She had extricated herself from him with difficulty.

When she drove back home with her Father, she did not tell him of her latest conquest.

Simon was a very wealthy young man who came from a good family.

She knew if she had wanted to marry him, the Earl would have raised no objections, and in fact would have been pleased about it.

As they had reached Strang House in Park Lane, Valeria had slipped her hand into her Father's.

"Now we can go to the country, Papa! Let us ride together as soon as we get there."

"We will do that," the Earl agreed, "but do not forget that we are leaving in two days for France, and I know you will be pleased when I tell you that I have arranged for us to go by sea."

Valeria gave a little cry of delight.

"Oh, Papa, how wonderful! It will be far nicer than going by train, and I always enjoy being on a yacht with you!"

"And I with you," the Earl said. "The sea at this time of the year should be reasonably calm, even in the Bay of Biscay."

"I rather enjoy it when it is rough," Valeria said, "as I know you do too. The battle against the elements is the most exciting battle of all."

The Earl laughed before he said:

"At least there are not so many casualties."

" 'Touch wood!' " his daughter said quickly. "We may sink to the bottom of the ocean to be eaten by the fishes."

"I shall be extremely annoyed if that happens to the *Sea Serpent!*" he said. "She has just been refitted and I am assured she is one of the soundest vessels afloat."

"That is certainly reassuring," Valeria said, "if at the same time slightly boring!"

The Earl laughed.

"If you are looking for danger, I would prefer it not to be at sea!"

"Then who knows? We may find it in Biarritz!"

Her Father laughed again.

Valeria was still thinking that to be in France would be an adventure, and perhaps very different from anything she had known in London.

"To be absolutely truthful," she said to herself, "London is boring, boring, and there is little chance of it being anything else."

Inevitably she asked herself what exactly she did want.

The answer was that she did not know.

She just knew that being grown up and being a *débutante* was not the thrill it should have been.

Something was missing; yet she did not know what she was seeking.

"Of one thing I am quite certain," she said as she turned from the wardrobe, "and that is it is not the *Duc* de Laparde!"

Marrying him, she thought, would be like taking a very high jump without knowing what was on the other side.

She walked to the window to look down on the well-laid-out garden with its green lawns and flower-filled beds.

They swept down to a lake beyond which was the Park with its ancient oak trees and spotted deer lying in the shadows of them.

It was very English, very beautiful, and very quiet.

Generations of women like herself had looked out of these windows.

Perhaps they had wanted adventure only to learn that the trees which had stood for hundreds of years would still be the same tomorrow.

Suddenly behind her her bedroom door was flung open and her brother Antony came tearing in.

"Quick, Valeria! Come quickly!" he said urgently. "Papa has had a fall, and I think he has broken a leg!"

Valeria turned from the window with a cry of horror.

Then she was following her brother down the stairs.

Coming through the front-door was her Father being carried by three grooms.

chapter two

VALERIA was upstairs in her bedroom, thinking that the clothes her maid had packed would have to be unpacked again.

She was not really sorry.

At the same time, she had looked forward to going to France with her Father.

The Earl was a very bad patient.

He was upsetting and disagreeable both to the Doctor and to the Nurse.

It was only by a miracle the latter was obtainable at such short notice.

Usually in the country there was no one to look after anyone who was ill except for the local Midwife.

She was traditionally reputed to keep going "on gin."

The local Doctor had with great dexterity produced an elderly woman who paid no attention to the Earl's grumbles and complaints.

She insisted on him lying in the position advised by the Doctor.

In actual fact, his leg was not as bad as they had at first anticipated.

It was not broken, only fractured, and he was bruised where he had fallen.

His horse had thrown him over his head at a high fence.

Valeria felt guilty.

It was she who had insisted that the jumps be heightened on what was almost a private Race-Course.

This had been done not once but several times so as to prove a challenge to Crusader.

"Poor Papa," she said to herself now, "he will be so disappointed not to see the *Duc*'s horses."

There was a knock on the door, and when she called, "Come in!" she saw it was her brother.

"Hello, Tony," she exclaimed, "I was just thinking of the bother it will be to unpack all the clothes I had chosen to take with me to France."

The Viscount came into the room and shut the door behind him.

"Listen, Vala," he said.

It was a nickname he had given his sister when he was a small boy, being unable to pronounce "Valeria."

He had never called her anything else.

He spoke now in such a conspiratorial manner that Valeria looked at him in surprise, and said:

"I am listening."

The Viscount glanced over his shoulder almost as if he thought somebody might be evesdropping.

Then he said:

"I have had the most marvellous, glorious idea, if only you will agree to it."

"Agree to what?" Valeria asked.

She sat down on the edge of the bed while her brother walked about as if he was agitated.

"I have just been talking to Papa," he said, "and he is upset that he cannot go to France with you as planned."

"I thought he would be," Valeria replied, "but we can go some other time."

"He thinks that would be a mistake, and he wants me to go in his place."

Valeria stared at her brother because it was something she had never contemplated for a moment.

Then she said:

"Why not! You are as keen on horses as Papa, but let us make it quite clear that is the only reason we are going."

Her brother laughed.

"That is what you think, but I am sure at the back of Papa's mind he is determined you shall not miss the opportunity of meeting the 'Awesome *Duc*'!"

"Awesome?" Valeria enquired.

"He must be from the way everybody talks about him," her brother answered. "They make a tremendous fuss over him in France—that I can understand, but your Grandmother speaks of him as if he were the Emperor Charlemagne!"

Valeria laughed.

"I suppose that is true, and the way she talks about the Château, it might be the Garden of Eden!"

"With the *Duc* as Adam, and you Eve!" Tony remarked.

"That will never happen," Valeria said quickly, "so put it out of your mind."

"What I have come to talk about is something quite different."

He sat down in the chair opposite her and said:

"Now, listen, for as far as I am concerned, this is the opportunity of a lifetime!"

"For what?"

"To see what I have always wanted to see, and that is the *Can-Can!*"

Valeria stared at him in astonishment.

"What can you mean? The *Can-Can* is in Paris."

"I know that," Tony said, "but I was talking to some of my friends in London and I mentioned that you and Papa were going to Biarritz, and what do you think they told me?"

"I have no idea."

"They said that the *Moulin Rouge* has been a huge success in Paris since it opened two years ago. And, as Biarritz is the most fashionable place in France at the moment, it has copied the *Moulin Rouge*. So the *Can-Can* is performed there!"

He sounded so excited at the idea that Valeria could only say:

"I suppose you could manage to see it while we are staying with the *Duc*."

"I think that is unlikely," Tony replied, "and you know, Vala, how I have begged Papa over and over again to let me go to Paris."

He made an expressive gesture with his hands as he said:

"It is too unfair! All the fellows of my age have

been to Paris to see the *Can-Can* and a great many other things as well. I feel such a dolt when I listen to them talking."

Valeria had heard all this before.

She knew that her Father had very firm ideas where Tony was concerned about where he should go and, for quite a number of reasons, Paris was barred to him.

She could understand that he would be very frustrated.

His friends with whom he had been at Oxford and spent his time in London made him feel, as he often said, like a "Country bumpkin."

Soothingly, because she did not want her brother to be upset, she said:

"I am sure you will have a chance to see the *Can-Can* while we are at the Château, but I doubt if Papa will let you and me stay for a few days in Biarritz."

"You can be quite certain of that!" her brother said quickly. "He has already told me I am to go with you to the Château, then come home immediately."

It was what Valeria might have expected, and she said only:

"Then there is really nothing you can do about it."

"But there is!" Tony argued. "And that is what I am trying to tell you."

"Well, make it clearer," Valeria replied, "because for the moment I can see no possible way of you enjoying the *Can-Can* unless the *Duc* wants to do the same."

"Why need he bother?" Tony asked. "He has a

house in Paris and he can go to Montmartre whenever he likes!"

There seemed to Valeria no point in remarking on the discrepancy between the *Duc*'s age and Tony's.

She was also concerned that the *Duc* was both stuck-up and grand, in which case he would not stoop to visit anything so vulgar as the entertainments that attracted younger men like Tony.

Because her brother had been frantically trying to visit France since he was eighteen, he talked continually of the nightlife in Paris.

Valeria felt she actually knew the Dance and Music Halls, the *Café-Concerts* and after it opened its doors in 1889, the *Moulin Rouge,* where the *Can-Can* had become world-famous.

It was Valeria's Grandmother who had told her that the *Can-Can* had originally been *le chahut*— a word signifying din and rumbustiousness.

The dance amused the working classes and was a remnant of the Franco-Prussian War.

"*Le chahut* took place," the Dowager Duchess said, "in very primitive surroundings. A wooden barrier separated the dance-floor from rough wooden tables where the audience drank pitchers of mulled wine."

"Did you ever go there, Grandmama?" Valeria asked.

"Of course not, *ma Petite!*" the Dowager Duchess replied. "What man could resist seeing women kicking their legs in the most immodest manner with a display of whirling petticoats and knickers not always as white as they should be!"

She obviously disapproved so violently that Valeria had been intrigued.

"Why did everybody talk about it?" she enquired.

The Dowager Duchess had thought for a moment. Then she said:

"I suppose really it was a challenge because the dance is a difficult one."

"Why?" Valeria asked.

"It required a great deal of training and physical agility, and became a spectacle which portrayed in one dance what everyone expected of 'Gay Paree.'"

She went on to explain, although she had never seen it, how the girls danced alone, without male partners.

They worked themselves up into a frenzy, spinning round like tops, and sometimes turning cartwheels.

"It must be very exciting, Grandmama!" Valeria remarked.

"I believe the most exciting moment," the Dowager Duchess replied, "is when the dancers spin on the toes of one foot while holding the other leg as high as possible with one hand."

"That is clever!" Valeria exclaimed.

"Another feature," the Dowager Duchess went on, "is *le grand écart,* or what the English call the splits."

"What was that?"

"The dancer would make a spectacular finish by ending on the floor with both legs outstretched completely horizontally."

Valeria clapped her hands.

"That sounds almost impossible."

"It is for any ordinary person," the Dowager Duchess said sharply, "and make no mistake, Valeria, it was a noisy, earthy, animal dance performed in an atmosphere of tobacco-smoke, sweat, and cheap perfume."

Although the Dowager Duchess sounded so scathing, Valeria had been intrigued.

She could therefore understand why Tony found it infuriating when all his friends could talk about the *Can-Can* and he had to admit he had never seen it.

She thought now that if the dance was being performed in Biarritz, then by hook or by crook, Tony would get there.

She knew, however, that it would be a mistake to encourage him.

Her Father would be furious if he upset the *Duc* or behaved in any way that was undignified.

Not to dampen his enthusiasm, she said:

"I expect something will work out."

"Only if you agree to do what I want," Tony replied.

"What do you want me to do?"

Again her brother looked over his shoulder towards the door before he said in a lowered voice:

"Papa told me to write to the *Duc* to say that he would unfortunately be unable to visit him as he had intended but that he was sending me in his place, and that I was greatly looking forward to seeing his horses."

"That sounds all right."

"What I have done," Tony said in an even lower voice, "is to change the dates."

Valeria stared at him.

"Why have you done that?"

"I have told the *Duc* that we will arrive on the

twentieth, but actually, unless everything goes wrong, we will reach Biarritz on the eighteenth."

Valeria stared at him.

"Do you mean . . . do you really mean that we will be there two days before the *Duc* is aware of it?"

"Exactly!" Tony said. "And for two nights, Valeria, I am going to watch the *Can-Can*."

"And . . . leave me alone?" Valeria enquired. "How can you be so unkind? And you know Papa would not approve of me staying alone on the yacht. What is more, the Captain would undoubtedly tell him what you had done."

"I have thought of that," Tony said, "and we will not be staying on the yacht."

"It would be worse in an Hôtel!" Valeria said. "And there would be even more fuss if you left me alone while you went out on the Town!"

"I have thought of that too," Tony said.

"And what is the solution?"

"That you will come with me to see the *Can-Can*."

"I do not believe you!" Valeria said. "How could I possibly do such a thing? And think of the row if it was discovered."

"It is not going to be discovered," Tony said, "because we are going to be very clever about it!"

"I cannot think how."

He smiled.

He had an expression in his eyes which had always been there since he was very small when he was doing something particularly naughty.

"You must realise, Tony," Valeria said quickly, "that I cannot do anything that would not only upset Papa but also Grandmama."

She paused a moment and then went on:

"She is so delighted that we are going to stay with her beloved *Duc,* and if we did anything like you are suggesting, I really think it would kill her."

"Nonsense!" Tony said. "Your Grandmother is French and the French understand these things."

"Well, I do not," Valeria retorted, "and my answer is 'No.' Therefore it is something you cannot do."

"If you will just listen to me for a moment," Tony said, "I will explain just how easy it can be."

Valeria raised her eye-brows, but she said nothing and her brother went on:

"We arrive at St. Jean de Luz on the eighteenth. That is the Port which I expect you know is only a few miles from Biarritz."

"I know that," Valeria agreed.

"The *Duc* is not expecting us, so there will be no one to see us stepping off the *Sea Serpent.* I shall instruct the Captain to anchor in a part of the Port where the yacht will not be noticed."

"Will he not think that strange?" Valeria asked.

"I will think up some good explanation," Tony replied.

"What do we do then?" Valeria enquired.

"We go to a small Hôtel which I have already heard about from one of my friends. It is not fashionable, but comfortable and very respectable. We will stay there for two nights."

Valeria parted her lips to say something, then thought it better to keep her protests until later.

"Once we are there," Tony went on, "you change into the smart clothes you will wear as the attractive widow, *Madame* Hérard."

Valeria stared at him.

"Are you mad? Why should I do that?"

"Because, my dear sister," Tony said, "you cannot watch the *Can-Can* as Lady Valeria Netherton, or the audience would be curious at seeing a pretty little *débutante* sitting amongst them."

"And you really think I can pretend to be a married woman?"

"You used to fancy yourself in those Charades we acted at Christmas. I remember you were a great success as one of Cinderella's Ugly Sisters."

"That was different," Valeria objected.

"Acting is acting," Tony replied, "and I do not imagine anyone is going to look at you when they can watch the *Can-Can*."

It was the sort of thing, Valeria thought, only a brother would say.

She laughed rather weakly.

"All you have to do," Tony went on, "is to look older than you really are and make up your face, as most Frenchwomen do, especially if they are attending anything so outrageous as a performance of the *Can-Can*."

"But . . . Grandmama said that no . . . *Lady* would ever . . . go to . . . such a place!"

There was a little pause, and Tony did not meet his sister's eyes as he said:

"I cannot imagine any of our relatives going there. At the same time, there are women, not perhaps of the *Beau Ton,* but nevertheless pretty and elegant, who would accompany a man on such an occasion."

He was choosing his words with care and speaking slowly.

Valeria suddenly exclaimed:

33

"Are you really suggesting, Tony, that I should pretend to be a *demi-mondaine*?"

"So you have heard of them!" Tony exclaimed.

"Of course I have heard of them!"

"From your Grandmother, I suppose."

"She has mentioned them from time to time, especially those in Paris who are so extravagant and on whom Englishmen as well as Frenchmen spend large fortunes."

"No one is likely to spend a large fortune on you," Tony said, "except me."

"You cannot be serious in what you are asking me to do!"

"Of course I am," he said, "otherwise you can stay alone in the Hôtel. I am not stopping you from doing that."

Valeria hesitated.

She could imagine nothing more depressing!

It would be miserable to be alone in some dull Hôtel, waiting hour after hour for Tony to return, flushed and excited by all he had seen.

She made one last attempt to save herself.

"Please, Tony," she begged, "do not do this. You know what a terrible row there would be if it was ever discovered, and Papa would never trust you again!"

"He does not trust me now!" Tony retorted. "When I suggested going to Paris for Easter, he said not for at least another year."

His voice sharpened as he continued:

"I said to him:

" 'Look, Papa, I am twenty-one and perfectly capable of looking after myself.' "

"What did Papa reply to that?" Valeria asked.

"He said:

" 'If you go to Paris without my approval, I will stop your allowance!'

"As I said at the time, it is not fair. I am not a child, but I am treated like one!"

"I know it is bad luck when you want so much to go to Paris," Valeria said. "At the same time, Papa did give you those two wonderful horses for Christmas, and you are going to Scotland in August."

"I know, I know," Tony agreed, "and one should be grateful for small mercies, but I am not going to Biarritz without seeing the *Can-Can*!"

He set his chin in a way which told his sister how determined he was.

She knew it was really no use going on arguing.

Whether she agreed or not, Tony would go and watch the *Can-Can*.

It was up to her, therefore, to choose whether she would go with him or stay alone in the Hôtel.

Quickly, because she disliked doing anything that would upset her Father, she said:

"You had better explain to me a little more clearly what it is you want me to do."

Tony gave a cry of delight.

"You agree? Oh, Vala, you are a sport! And I promise you it will be the greatest fun we have ever had!"

"I hope so," Valeria said. "But I am frightened Papa may find out."

"I will take good care that he does not," Tony said, "and he will never know if we do exactly what I have arranged."

"You will tell me what I am to wear when I am pretending to be *Madame*—what was her name?"

"*Madame* Hérard," Tony repeated.

"I only hope I can remember it!"

"Of course you will, and you can remain 'Vala,' which nobody calls you but me. It sounds almost French, like your real name."

Valeria had been christened after an obscure Saint who was actually Italian and supposedly the wife of St. Vitis.

The name had been very popular in Italy and also in France.

After she had been born her Mother had insisted that it was the name she wanted for her daughter.

However, to please the Netherton family, Valeria was also christened more traditionally Mary and Adelaide.

It was true that only Tony called her "Vala."

Although it was unlikely anyone would ask who she was, she was afraid she might be taken by surprise and answer "Valeria Netherton."

"Very well," she said. "I am *Madame* Hérard, and what do you want me to wear?"

"Something smart, and something which makes you look much older than you do at the moment," Tony replied.

Valeria looked hopelessly at the open door of her wardrobe.

As was correct for a *débutante,* nearly every gown was white with the exception of a few very soft pinks and blues.

There was certainly nothing at all sophisticated about them.

"It is hopeless . . . !" she began.

Suddenly she gave a cry.

"I have just thought of something!"

"What is it?" Tony asked.

"Cousin Gwendolyn left quite a lot of clothes here before she went to Africa."

"Gwendolyn always looks very smart," Tony remarked.

Their cousin was nearly thirty, and had the reputation in London of always dressing in the height of fashion.

Her husband had for a long time been wishing to go on safari in Africa.

They had therefore left England, intending to travel for at least three months.

"Her clothes are still where she left them in the Lilac Room," Valeria said now. "I can borrow one or two and I am sure I can pack them myself without Emily being aware of it."

"Now you are beginning to see sense," Tony said.

"There is nothing sensible about it," his sister replied, "but I have no wish to be exposed as an impostor!"

"I assure you there will be nobody where we are going who will want to do that," Tony said, "and do not forget that you will also want hats for the evening."

"Hats?" Valeria exclaimed.

Then, before her brother could reply, she said:

"Yes, of course! Grandmama told me that nearly all Frenchwomen wear hats in the evening. It seems strange that no one does so in London."

"You have to look French," Tony said, "and at least you can talk the lingo like a native!"

"I should hope so," his sister answered. "Grandmama would be furious if I spoke anything but

37

the purest Parisien, and Mama was very particular too."

"I know enough to get what I want," Tony said, "but I used to see your Mother wince when I pronounced a word the wrong way."

Valeria laughed.

She could remember the many arguments when they were small as her Mother tried to make Tony speak good French.

However hard she tried, he always retained his English accent.

Aloud she said:

"I had better go and fetch Cousin Gwendolyn's clothes from her room this evening, when the maids are all downstairs having supper."

"You will need something for the daytime too," Tony reminded her. "If you are staying in the Hôtel as *Madame* Hérard, you can hardly come down the stairs looking completely different from when you went up!"

"I will do my best not to shame you," Valeria said, "but at the same time, I think the whole idea is crazy, and I shall be terrified the whole time lest Papa or the *Duc* find out. Then we shall both be blown sky high!"

"Leave everything to me," Tony said loftily. "I am quite sure you will enjoy the *Can-Can* as much as I will!"

Valeria resisted an impulse to say that was impossible.

She could not, however, help thinking that it would be very exciting to see something she had heard so much about.

She had never expected to see it.

The *Can-Can* had caught the imagination not only of France but also of other countries as well.

From the way people talked, and not only her Grandmother, it seemed it was part of the great myth of Paris.

The City had become the "World Capital of Erotic Pleasure."

She could understand her Father's determination to keep Tony, who was very impressionable, away from Paris.

But she was also sympathetic towards her brother because he felt humiliated in front of his friends.

"I am sure it would be best if I kept with him," she argued to herself, "and go with him to this place. He might get into all sorts of trouble if he goes alone, and he would have no one to turn to for help."

At the same time, it was a rather frightening thought.

*   *   *

When later that evening Valeria slipped along to the Lilac Room, she was still wishing she could persuade Tony to change his mind.

There were so many bedrooms in Strang House that the one her cousin had occupied when she had last stayed with them had remained untouched.

Her clothes were where she had left them.

Her gold dressing-table set with her initials in diamonds was still in place.

She had also left some pretty and obviously expensive *ombrelles*.

When Valeria opened the wardrobe doors, there was a kaleidoscope of brilliant colours.

It seemed extraordinary that Cousin Gwendolyn could manage to be properly attired in Africa without the gowns she had left behind.

As one of the smartest ladies in London, it was not surprising that she should have so many clothes.

Valeria suspected that when she returned she would say they were all out-of-date.

She concentrated first on the evening-gowns, wondering in which she would look the most sophisticated.

Finally she chose one in black which had obviously come from Paris.

It was certainly not the dowdy black which one associated with mourning.

It had little touches of white transparent chiffon which revealed rather than concealed the chest.

There was a swirl of frills round the hem.

When Valeria put it on, she thought that if nothing else, she certainly did not look like a *débutante*.

The other gown she chose was a deep midnight blue.

It was ornamented with diamanté which were like stars and glittered when she moved.

She thought the décolletage looked rather low, although it had seemed all right on Cousin Gwendolyn.

She supposed no one in Biarritz would expect her to be very modest.

The shelf of the wardrobe was filled with a variety of hats.

Valeria discarded those with wide brims or thick crowns.

Finally she found what she was sure would meet with Tony's approval.

It was a swirl of feathers which encircled her head.

The blue gown was rather more difficult to match.

There was a small toque again trimmed with feathers.

They shaded from pale blue to dark and were eventually the same colour as the gown.

Valeria found two gowns each with small boleros for the daytime with two matching hats.

Then she hurried back to her bedroom.

She packed the hats beneath her own, and the gowns she had chosen she put in her trunk and closed the lid.

She fastened the straps, which was really the job of the footmen.

As she finished, she felt as if she were part of some great conspiracy.

She could not help knowing it would be worse when they reached Biarritz.

"How can Tony have thought of anything so dangerous?" she asked herself.

Then she thought she was being unnecessarily cowardly.

The *Duc* would not be expecting them until two days later.

In any case, he would certainly not be worrying about her.

The more she thought about the *Duc*, the more she thought it was a ridiculous idea on her Grandmother's part.

How could she marry a man who was so much older than herself?

What was more, he had apparently already tasted all the delights that the world could offer him in the way of wine, women, and love.

Her Grandmother was constantly talking about him.

She knew that as Head of the Family he had a very special place in their hearts.

It was not really comparable to anything the English felt about their family.

It was true that everybody respected her Father.

Of course, his relations consulted him when they were in trouble.

But the French seemed to think of the Head of the Family as some God-like creature who commanded their whole destiny.

"The way Grandmama speaks of the *Duc* makes me feel as if he has come from another Planet altogether," Valeria said to herself scornfully, "and I should approach him on my knees!"

Then she laughed, because she knew it was her English blood which was rebelling at something that was traditionally French.

Because she resented the *Duc*'s ascendancy over his family, it was amusing to think that, in doing what Tony wanted, she was, although he would never know of it, defying him.

'He is obviously too puffed up with his own importance to imagine that any of his relations could do anything but *salaam* as if he were an Eastern Potentate!' she thought. 'Well, in defying the conventions, I shall be scoring a point on their behalf.'

As she got into bed she decided she was no longer frightened of what Tony had persuaded her to do.

'We are leading a small revolution all on our own,' she thought. 'Tony and I against the "Awesome *Duc*"!'

chapter three

IT was the night before they were leaving for France.

Valeria suddenly realised she had not found the cosmetics that Tony had ordered her to use.

When he had spoken of it she remembered they had some sort of grease-paint and make-up for the Charades.

She suspected they were somewhere in the attic with the Fancy Dress Costumes.

Now she wondered if they had dried up or else been thrown away.

'Tony will be furious,' she thought, 'and there will be no time to buy anything before we embark on the yacht.'

Then she wondered if once again her cousin Gwendolyn might come to the rescue.

She waited until everyone was asleep, then crept down the corridor to the bedroom from where she had taken Gwendolyn's clothes.

As she had seen before, her brushes and combs were still on the dressing-table.

There was also a bottle of exotic French perfume and one or two other gold-topped bottles.

None of these seemed to be much use, so she opened a drawer.

There she found a box of face powder and two powder-puffs.

That was a start, but there seemed to be nothing else.

Then, as she put her hand right to the back of the drawer, she found a box.

When she opened it she found it contained a small pot of salve.

This, she thought, could be used both on her lips and on her cheeks.

It had come from a very expensive shop.

It was not the brilliant rather vulgar red which had been used on Tony when her Mother was making him up as a Clown.

"Now I have all I want!" Valeria said to herself.

Then she saw there was another smaller box beside the salve, and opened it curiously.

To her surprise, she saw it contained mascara.

She had never imagined that any Lady would use mascara, although she was aware that it was used by actresses.

Her Mother had put some on her eye-lashes to make her look grotesque for her role as one of the Ugly Sisters in *Cinderella*.

She looked at the mascara and the little brush that went with it and thought:

'If I am to look like a real *demi-mondaine,* I am sure I should use mascara.'

Looking back, she remembered she had always been very impressed by Cousin Gwendolyn's long dark eye-lashes.

They had seemed particularly long in the evenings.

"Fancy Cousin Gwendolyn being so dashing!" she said with a smile.

At the same time, she was not really surprised.

As her cousin had grown older, she had become more and more fussy about her appearance.

She had never been a great beauty like her Mother.

But men admired her, and she certainly looked smarter than most of their relatives.

"I will take the salve and the mascara with me," Valeria decided.

She picked them up, also the powder and the puffs.

Then she crept back to her own room and hid her spoils in the bottom of her dressing-case.

The next morning Valeria went to say goodbye to the Earl.

He was still in bed and still, as he said angrily, in pain.

"It is so disappointing, Papa, that you are not coming with me!" Valeria said.

"I know, my dearest," he answered, "but we will go together another time, and I am sure Tony will talk intelligently about the *Duc*'s horses."

"But it will not be the same as being with you," Valeria insisted.

She kissed him.

As Tony had already left the room to go downstairs to see to the luggage, the Earl said:

"Look after your brother, Valeria, and see that he does not get into mischief."

Valeria felt guiltily that that was what he was doing already.

There was, however, nothing she could do about it.

"I will do my best, Papa," she promised.

"And come straight back home as soon as your visit to the Château is finished," her Father said firmly.

It was almost as if he had a premonition of what Tony was planning.

Quickly Valeria kissed him again and went downstairs to where Tony was waiting for her.

They got into the carriage which was waiting to take them to the station, as they were to travel to Folkestone by train.

It was there that the Earl kept his yacht in harbour ready for when he needed it.

It was a long time since Valeria had been at sea.

She knew as soon as they got into a Reserved Carriage that Tony was very excited.

"We are off!" he exclaimed. "I could not sleep last night for thinking that something might go wrong at the last moment which would prevent us from leaving."

"I only hope that when we get to Biarritz you will not be disappointed," Valeria replied.

"I believe the *Moulin de la Mer* is equally as good as the *Moulin Rouge*," Tony answered.

"*Moulin de la Mer*, 'Windmill of the Sea'—that is

a very pretty name!" Valeria remarked.

"And from all I have been told, it is a very pretty show," Tony said, "and now Papa cannot prevent me from seeing the *Can-Can*."

His boyish enthusiasm was so infectious that Valeria was really worried in case it did not come up to his expectations.

"There will be a lot to see at the Château, I expect," she reminded him, "the *Duc*'s horses, for one."

"I know," Tony remarked, "and Papa gave me quite a lecture on them. Apparently the *Duc* has won all the major races in France!"

"All you need to do is praise them. He certainly will not expect any criticism."

She was sure the *Duc* would resent anyone as young as Tony thinking that there was anything about his stables that was not perfect.

As if Tony was following her thoughts without her saying them aloud, he said:

"If you ask me, the 'Awesome *Duc*' has too much of everything, and it must be bad for him."

"Can one really have too much of the best things in life?" Valeria asked just to be argumentative.

"Of course, when it is somebody else who has them!" Tony retorted.

Because it was such an obvious answer, they both laughed.

It was a tiring journey to Folkestone because they had to change trains.

The Earl had insisted on sending a Courier with them so that they did not have to bother with the luggage.

A compartment had also been reserved in the

train which was to take them right down to the harbour.

The *Sea Serpent* was looking magnificent, and as they stepped aboard they were welcomed by the Captain.

"Nice to see you, M'Lady!" he greeted Valeria. "And you too, M'Lord. It's too long since we were honoured by Your Lordship's presence."

"Through no fault of mine, I assure you," Tony replied. "I have wanted to visit France for a long time."

"Well, we've a fine day for it," the Captain remarked cheerily, "and as soon as Your Lordship gives the orders, we can leave."

"Then do so immediately," Tony replied. "Quite frankly, Captain Bennett, I am in a hurry to get to St. Jean de Luz."

"Then we must certainly try to break all records," the Captain promised.

The furnishings of the *Sea Serpent* had been originally chosen by Valeria's Mother and were very attractive.

The Saloon was in shades of jade green with touches of pink on the cushions.

Valeria's cabin, which had originally been occupied by her mother, was in pink.

It had attractively flowered curtains to cover the port-holes.

Tony, as a matter of right, occupied the Master Cabin, which was where his Father usually slept.

It was very much more masculine, the largest cabin, and had its own shower.

"This is what I call comfort!" Tony said when they were both inspecting it. "As you can guess, I have never been allowed to sleep here before!"

"Then make the most of it!" Valeria said. "If Papa finds out what you have been up to, I doubt if he will ever let you put to sea again."

"Do not try to frighten me," Tony said, "we have started out on our 'Voyage of Discovery,' and it is no use turning back."

He spoke in a tone of triumph.

Valeria realised they had in fact left the harbour and were already in the open sea.

She went up on deck and watched the waves as the sun began to sink in a blaze of glory.

She thought nothing could be more beautiful, or in fact more exciting.

She was looking forward to being in France and in a part she had never visited before.

She had several times crossed the Channel with her mother to stay with her French relatives who lived in Normandy.

She had been quite small when she first went there.

With every succeeding visit she found herself becoming more and more enamoured with the beautiful country.

She loved the long straight roads with the tall trees standing like sentinels on each side of them.

She loved the picturesque hamlets and ancient Churches.

She would watch the peasants as they worked industriously in the fields.

"I love France," she told herself as she stood at the railing of the *Sea Serpent,* "but I also love England. I am very fortunate to belong to two such beautiful countries."

She had the feeling, as the yacht proceeded down Channel, that she was doing something momentous, in fact, something she had never done before.

She was sure she felt like that only because Tony was making it such an adventure.

Yet her instinct was never wrong.

This was more than an ordinary visit from one relative to another.

The Chef abroad the yacht was a Frenchman who had been chosen by Valeria's Mother.

The dinner he provided for them in the Saloon was delicious.

When it was over, Tony went up on the bridge while Valeria went to her cabin.

"I am tired," she said to her brother. "I nearly forgot the make-up you insisted I should wear and I had to stay awake last night until it was safe for me to go to Cousin Gwendolyn's room and borrow what she had left behind."

"Thank God you thought of it!" Tony exclaimed. "I suppose you remembered a wedding-ring?"

"I have brought Mama's, which fortunately fits me exactly," Valeria replied. "I have also brought some of her jewellery with me."

"Now, that was clever of you!" Tony said approvingly. "I never thought of it, but of course *Madame* Hérard would be wearing ear-rings and a flashy necklace."

"Which is what she will wear," Valeria replied, "so you need not be ashamed of her."

Tony put his hand round his sister's shoulders.

"As I said before, you are a jolly good sport, Vala, and you have also been very kind to me."

"It will be all right so long as nobody ever discovers what we have done," Valeria said.

"I will make sure of that," Tony boasted. "And you may be quite certain we are not likely to see any of your relations in the *Moulin de la Mer*."

"I hope not," Valeria said fervently. "Think how shocked they would be, and they would certainly rush home to tell Papa!"

"None of that is going to happen," Tony said confidently. "The only difficulty is going to be not to talk of the experience when we return and say how much we have enjoyed it."

"I, at any rate, will be very careful," Valeria promised. "But if there is any trouble, you will be blamed because you are the elder." ·

"If you say any more, I will lock you in the wardrobe while I go off to the *Moulin* by myself," Tony threatened, "and release you only when I return."

"I promise I will be well behaved and do exactly as you tell me," Valeria said in a voice of mock humility.

Tony kissed her.

"Go to bed, Vala," he said, "and dream about anyone except the 'Awesome *Duc*.' He is bound to be an Ogre, or the Demon King. We do not have to deal with him, thank Heavens, until the twentieth." ·

* * *

The next day the sea was considerably rougher than it had been before.

As Valeria had told her Father, she enjoyed a battle with the elements, and she spent most of her time on deck watching the waves break over the bow.

Both she and Tony were very good sailors, and

neither of them felt in the least seasick.

By mid-morning the sea was very rough.

They had to move about very carefully in case they should slip and break an arm or a leg.

"If we have to turn about and return to England," Tony said, "I shall either burst into tears, or else throw you overboard!"

"I am being very careful," Valeria promised, "and you do the same. I do not suppose the *Duc* wants an invalid on his hands."

"He would certainly find that a bore," Tony said, "and doubtless return immediately to Paris, leaving me at the mercy of a number of your aged relations."

"They might be beautiful and fascinating like Mama," Valeria protested.

"They say that lightning never strikes in the same place twice!" Tony replied. "Your Mother was beautiful and also, I am quite certain, exceptional."

Valeria thought this was certainly true of her Mother's relatives who lived in Normandy.

They had been pleasant and kind with compassionate faces, but none of them had her Mother's exceptional beauty.

She was certainly very lucky that she had some of it herself, at least her Mother's blue eyes, which as her Father had often said, seemed to sparkle even in the darkness.

"Are you suggesting I have eyes like a cat?" her mother had asked once.

"No, my darling, like a star."

Valeria could always remember how her Mother had smiled at the compliment and kissed her Father on the cheek.

"As long as I can light and guide you," she said, "you know I am content."

"That is what you always do," he answered softly.

Her eyes were like her Mother's, and they were, in fact, almost identical.

What Valeria had inherited from her English relations was her delicate pink-and-white English skin, and her hair, which was not dark like her Mother's.

But it was also not fair, but the deep gold that was not only English, but was also to be found in Normandy.

It made her look very different both from English and French girls.

In fact, although she hardly realised it herself, she had been a sensation from the moment she made her curtsy at Buckingham Palace.

When she appeared at the first Ball to which she was invited in London at Devonshire House, she had been showered with compliments.

The Earl had certainly been very proud of her, and so had her Grandmother.

"You are more French than English, my dearest," she said to Valeria, "whatever your Father may say."

"I am delighted to be both," Valeria had replied, "but I expect English people find me too French and the French will find me too English."

She had laughed as she spoke.

She did not realise it was at that moment that it suddenly struck the Dowager Duchess that she might captivate the elusive *Duc*.

She had almost despaired of him every marrying again.

It had therefore never occurred to her that Valeria, whom she loved very deeply, might be the answer.

From that moment she began, like a busy spider, to spin a web in which she hoped that the *Duc* and Valeria might be caught.

She had been very eloquent and at the same time very tactful with the Earl, who was actually very fond of her.

"I suppose it is to be expected, George," she said, "that you, who are so handsome, and my daughter, who was so beautiful, would produce anything so lovely as Valeria."

"She has certainly been a great success," the Earl agreed.

He spoke somewhat warily.

Although he was devoted to his mother-in-law, he knew only too well how she would use every possible persuasion in order to get her own way.

As the Dowager Duchess went on talking, it soon became clear to the Earl what it was she wanted.

"Do you really think, *Belle-mère,*" he asked, "that Valeria, who is only eighteen, could possibly cope with somebody like de Laparde, who to say the least of it, is a Roué."

"Valeria may be young," the Dowager Duchess replied, "but she is very intelligent, and although you may not be aware of it, extremely clever in her understanding and appreciation of people."

"I am aware of it," the Earl replied.

"It could, of course, come from her French blood," the Dowager Duchess said decisively.

"She will need that and a great deal more if she is to marry de Laparde," the Earl replied, "and quite frankly, I think he would make her unhappy."

"Claudius has behaved as he has in the last few years only because his wife was mad," the Dowager Duchess said. "Would you expect him to have done anything else in his efforts to forget that insane creature?"

The Dowager Duchess's eyes flashed, and her voice was hard as she said:

"I will never forgive the girl's parents for allowing her to marry any man, let alone *mon pauvre* Claudius. I only hope that when they die, they find themselves in the sort of Hell that he has endured!"

The Earl knew how bitterly the Dowager Duchess felt on the subject, and therefore said quickly:

"All I want for Valeria is that she should be happy, and you, of all people, know how I felt about her Mother."

"There is no doubt you made Yvonne the happiest woman in the world," the Dowager Duchess conceded, "but now, dear George, be guided by me and let us arrange that Claudius at least meets Valeria, then leave the rest in the hands of the gods."

She gave him a little smile before she added:

"Or, rather, to my prayers."

There was nothing the Earl could do but agree.

He therefore wrote to the *Duc* and suggested that he should visit him at his Château and take Valeria with him.

Never could he have anticipated that when everything was arranged he, who was an outstanding horseman, should have a fall, a mishap which would keep him in his bed for at least a month.

*　*　*

As the *Sea Serpent* pitched and tossed, Valeria was thinking how sorry she was for her Father.

And yet perhaps it was fate that Tony should take his place.

"At least after this," she told herself before she went to sleep, "we will have to hear no more complaints about him not having seen the *Can-Can* and that is the really important point about this visit, although nobody must know except us."

*　*　*

The next day the sea was still rough and subsided only as they ran down the coast towards St. Jean de Luz.

She knew the Captain's calculations had been upset.

Instead of arriving at the Port early in the morning as he had planned, they did not dock until nearly seven o'clock.

Tony instructed the Captain to berth in a part of the Port that was not frequented by a large number of foreign vessels.

As they arrived at the Quay, Valeria knew that Tony was in an agitated state.

She, however, while in the yacht, had read several books about St. Jean de Luz and its history.

It fascinated her to learn that the sailors of the Port had been the first to fish the Grand Banks of Newfoundland.

Their ships formed the greater part of the force which relieved the English blockade at La Rochelle in 1627.

It was the sort of thing she liked to know about any place she was visiting.

Tony, however, whose one ambition was to see the *Can-Can,* would not discuss it with her.

"Do you not realise," she asked, "that the transference of the Newfoundland fishing rights to England in 1713 was a bitter blow from which St. Jean never recovered?"

Tony was not listening.

"You will have to change quickly," he said. "The first Show at the *Moulin* starts at nine o'clock, and if we are not there promptly, we may not get a good table."

"What is a 'good table'?" Valeria asked.

"As near the performers as possible," Tony replied.

"I am sure there is plenty of time," she murmured.

He did not answer.

She looked up to try to see the turreted *Maison de l'Infanta.*

Her book told her it was where Marie-Theresa lodged before her marriage with Louis XIV.

It was always thrilling to see part of French History which she had learnt mostly from her Mother and Grandmother.

She told herself it was understandable that Tony was not interested.

He had no French blood in him, so why should he be concerned with a country which for many years had been an enemy of England?

"Come along, come along!" he was saying. "I cannot think why a country where the people speak so fast should move so slowly!"

Valeria thought it better not to argue.

She hurriedly indicated to the seamen which of her trunks she wanted put ashore and which were to remain on board.

She had carefully repacked the things she would need as *Madame* Hérard when she joined the *Sea Serpent*.

The rest she left for when she reached the Château.

She only hoped she had forgotten nothing.

Tony was hustling her towards the carriage he had hired and their luggage was already being heaped up behind them.

The horses drove off.

Because there were only two of them, Valeria was quite certain that Tony would complain they were moving too slowly long before they reached Biarritz.

"We are here," she said as they left the Quay, "and I am sure everything is going to be very exciting!"

"We should have started earlier for Folkestone," Tony said in a disagreeable tone. "I had no idea the sea could be so rough at this time of the year!"

"I am sure there is plenty of time," Valeria said soothingly. "It is not yet half-past-seven."

"We will not get to Biarritz before eight," Tony complained, "and I suppose you will take an eternity to change your clothes."

"I will be very quick, I promise you," Valeria answered. "At the same time, as I have to do a lot of strange things to my face, there would be no point in making a mess of it."

"No, of course not," Tony agreed, "but please,

Vala, hurry. It would be too awful if, when we got there, we could not get in."

"I am sure that will not happen," Valeria replied.

When they reached what appeared to be a pleasant Hôtel on the outskirts of Biarritz, she hurried up to the rooms which Tony had booked in advance.

She did not even give herself time to look at her surroundings.

She could see there was a garden bright with flowers in which a small fountain was playing.

This told her that, if nothing else, it would be quiet at night with no wheels or the clatter of hoofs to keep them awake.

Tony had engaged a bedroom for her to which was added a small Sitting-Room.

There was a bedroom for him on the other side of it.

They were not large, but comfortably furnished, and as Valeria saw at a glance, spotlessly clean.

She knew that was something she could always expect in France.

Her Mother had told her it was characteristic of the whole country.

Her trunk was brought up to her bedroom, and as soon as Tony had tipped the Porters he said:

"Now hurry, hurry! And do not forget—you must wear a hat."

"I have not forgotten," Valeria replied. "Now go away and get yourself changed, and you had better order something to eat."

She thought as she spoke that it would have been wise to have had something before they left the yacht.

It was too late now.

As Tony left the room she hurriedly lifted Cousin Gwendolyn's evening-gown from her trunk.

Valeria had already practised arranging her hair in a more elaborate manner than the way she wore it as a *débutante*.

However, it would not show, she thought, under the feathered hat she was wearing.

She therefore pinned it up as swiftly as she could.

The feathers swept over her forehead and out at the sides in what she thought was a very sophisticated manner.

She then opened the little boxes which belonged to her cousin Gwendolyn.

She put some rouge on her fingers, then rubbed it into her cheeks.

She powdered her face as she had seen her mother do before she went to a Ball.

Then came the difficult part of applying mascara to her already long, dark eye-lashes.

She put just a touch of mascara on the little brush.

But the effect was to make her lashes even longer and certainly more obvious.

"I hope it is not too much," Valeria worried, drawing a little nearer to the mirror.

She reddened her lips before she stepped into her gown.

As she had anticipated, she could not fasten it herself and rang for a chambermaid.

The woman buttoned up her gown and also helped Valeria to fasten her jewellery.

She had brought diamond ear-rings belonging to her mother and a diamond necklace that went with them.

They were not as spectacular or as valuable as those belonging to the Netherton-Strangeways collections.

Those her Mother wore only on very special occasions.

The necklace gave an added smartness to her appearance which seemed to sweep away any resemblance to a young and innocent *débutante*.

She put her Mother's wedding-ring on her finger, then added another which consisted of five graduated diamonds.

She then put on the bracelet her Mother had always worn.

It was the first of many presents the Earl had given her.

Valeria had also remembered she needed gloves.

There were some black ones in one of the drawers in her cousin's bedroom.

She had nearly forgotten a wrap until she recalled that she herself had one of her Mother's.

It was made of black velvet and trimmed with sable.

She thought it would be too hot, but she decided to take it with her in any case.

She had just finished and was looking at the effect in the mirror, when Tony came in.

"Surely you are ready by now," he exclaimed. "Goodness knows why women take so long!"

Valeria turned round and he stared at her.

"D-do I . . . look all right?" she asked.

"You look wonderful! Absolutely wonderful!" he said. "And exactly as I wanted you to look. Now, come on! There is no time to waste. The carriage is outside and it is nearly a quarter to nine!"

He escorted Valeria down the stairs and handed her into the carriage.

He tipped the Porter and the man said:

"Merci beaucoup, Monsieur!"

The carriage door closed, and as they started off, Valeria said:

"I never asked you—in fact I have only just thought of it—what name you are using. I know mine."

"I thought I had already told you," Tony replied.

"No, and I have no idea if you are French or English."

"I know what you think of my French," Tony said with a wry smile, "so I am English. Antony Archer—at your service!"

"Why 'Archer'?"

"I thought it sounded rather well," Tony explained, "and also it is the name of one of my friends."

"I am sure he will not mind you borrowing it for the occasion."

"Not if he saw you!" Tony exclaimed. "Honestly, Vala, I do not believe even your Grandmother would recognise you dressed like that!"

"I hope not!" Valeria said. "And mind you admire my mascaraed eye-lashes."

"The whole 'get-up' looks absolutely splendid!" Tony said admiringly. "And do not forget you are supposed to be my *chère amie,* otherwise I would not be taking you to the *Moulin*."

Valeria stared at him.

"Your *chère amie*?" she repeated. "Do you really mean that?"

"Of course," Tony said. "It is what is expected. And if you were not with me, I would be expected to be hospitable to one of the women who are there."

"You mean they provide men with partners if they need them?"

"Of course," Tony said, "but they will not trouble if you are with me, and all I want to do is to watch the *Can-Can*."

He spoke in a somewhat irritable manner, so Valeria did not pursue the subject.

She thought it was all very puzzling and something she had not anticipated.

As she had expected, he was already complaining as she looked out of the windows, that the horses were slow.

Because she did not want to think too much of what lay ahead, Valeria tried to have her first glimpse of Biarritz.

Her Grandmother had told her quite a lot about it.

She knew it had become fashionable because Eugénie de Montijo, the Spanish Beauty who had become Empress of France, had often visited Biarritz when she was a girl.

Then she had persuaded Napoleon III to accompany her to the Basque Coast for the first time in 1854.

The following year the Emperor, as fascinated by the place as his wife, had constructed a residence— the Villa Eugénie.

It was due to them and all the famous people who followed them that Biarritz had become more and more fashionable.

Through the windows Valeria could see there

were a number of large buildings, some of them Hôtels.

There were others under construction.

She wanted to talk about it all to Tony.

But he was obviously counting the minutes until they reached the *Moulin*.

It was with a sigh of relief that Valeria realised that at last they were there.

As the horses came to a standstill, she said:

"Here we are, and now you will be happy!"

"And about time!" Tony snapped.

He jumped out of the carriage as a resplendent Commissionaire came to open it.

It was then, revolving above their heads, that Valeria saw the arms of the Windmill.

'It must look very similar to the *Moulin Rouge* in Montmartre,' she thought.

'We are here—we are here at last!' she wanted to cry.

Then she looked a little apprehensively at the crowd of men pouring in through the open doors.

chapter four

TONY pushed his way through the crowd, and Valeria had difficulty in following him.

Inside, there was a large hall, and it seemed to her that the tables, and there were a great number of them, were all occupied.

With a sudden sinking of her heart she thought that if after all this Tony could not see the *Can-Can* it would be a disaster.

Then she realised that he was forcing his way towards a man who was obviously the *Maître d'Hôtel*.

He was directing people to the different tables as they arrived.

She reached Tony's side just as he had put a note of a very large denomination into the man's hand and was saying:

"I want a good table as near as possible."

The *Maître d'Hôtel* glanced down at the note and said in a respectful tone:

"*Merci, Monsieur,* I'm sure I can accommodate you."

He led the way forward to where Valeria could now see there were two empty tables.

They were right on the edge of the dance-floor.

To her relief, they were led towards one of them.

Almost as soon as they sat down, the one next to them was also filled.

Tony sat back in his chair with what was obviously a deep sigh of satisfaction.

"We are here!" he said.

Valeria was looking round her.

The place was much more elaborately decorated than her Grandmother had intimated.

Behind the dance-floor there was an attractive and modern-looking drop-scene.

Rising slightly, the hall had a long Bar which ran the whole length of the opposite wall.

Valeria realised that all the men occupying the tables were in evening dress.

With them were young women as made up as she was herself.

She could also see a number of unaccompanied women standing in front of the Bar.

Men were smoking, and on every table there was a bottle of champagne.

She was not surprised when Tony ordered one and a waiter brought it immediately.

"I would like some mineral water, if it is possible," she said to Tony.

He called the waiter back and ordered what she required.

"Can we have anything to eat here?" she asked.

He was looking around the room, and he did not appear at first to have heard what she said:

Then he answered vaguely:

"Oh, I expect so later, but the performance will begin in a few minutes, so I am sure it will be difficult to get anything until it is over."

Valeria realised that was true and therefore lapsed into silence as she continued to look round the room.

This, at any rate, was an experience that she would never have again.

The Band had begun to play, and she was aware that everyone was looking towards the dance-floor.

Lights lit up on each side of it.

The conversation seemed to be dying down, and all the tables were taken.

"We were only just in time," Valeria said to herself.

At that moment the *Maître d'Hôtel* came up to the table, and behind him was a man and a woman.

"*Pardon, Monsieur,*" he said to Tony, "but I am afraid this table was engaged by *Monsieur le Comte* de Savin. I am very sorry to incommode you, but I will try to find you another as soon as possible."

Tony looked up at the *Maître d'Hôtel,* and Valeria saw the fury in his eyes.

"Now, look here," he said, "I paid you well to have this table, and I am not moving for anyone!"

He was speaking in French, but with a strong British accent.

Nevertheless, the *Maître d'Hôtel,* like Valeria, realised that he was intending to be truculent.

67

She thought it would be embarrassing to have a scene.

She was also aware that the people round them were staring, and she put her hand on Tony's arm and said in a low voice:

"Please, Tony, do not make any trouble."

"The trouble is not of my making," Tony replied, "and I refuse, utterly refuse, to move."

It was then the man behind the *Maître d'Hôtel* came forward.

Without meaning to do so, Valeria looked up at him pleadingly.

"I think," he said in a very refined French voice, "we can settle this dispute quite amicably if we share the table. I did, in fact, engage it, but as I am slightly late, the *Maître d'Hôtel* assumed that I would not be coming here this evening."

"That is very kind of you, *Monsieur le Comte*," Valeria said before Tony could reply.

Then, as there was a roll of drums, without saying anything more the *Comte* sat down at the table.

He was beside Valeria, and the woman with him sat on his other side next to Tony.

As they did so there was a second roll of drums and the lights rose even higher.

A man came out onto the centre of the floor, and as he began to speak Valeria said to the *Comte*:

"Thank you, thank you very much."

He looked at her with what she thought was an amused twist to his lips as he replied:

"It obviously means a great deal to your friend to see the *Can-Can*."

Valeria nodded.

"It is something to which he has been looking

forward so much that it would have been a tragedy if we had to miss seeing it at the last moment."

"Then I am glad I have been able to avoid anything so disastrous," the Frenchman said.

There was a somewhat sarcastic note in his voice.

Valeria thought he was laughing at them for being what Tony would have called "Country bumpkins."

Yet all that mattered was that the crisis was over.

Tony had already turned round to face the dance-floor so that he almost had his back to her.

A waiter arrived with a bottle of champagne for the *Comte*.

It was obvious he had brought him a different Vintage from the bottle which he had provided for Tony.

She glanced at it and thought it was the sort of champagne her Father drank.

The *Comte,* sensing her interest, said:

"I hope you will join me in what is one of the best wines obtainable in this place, and I strongly advise you not to drink anything out of the bottle which they have left for you."

Valeria smiled.

"As I had never heard of it, I rather anticipated that it would have come from an inferior Vineyard."

"It does not come from a Vineyard of any sort!" the *Comte* said. "I am sure, *Madame,* you are experienced enough to know that the average man who comes here to watch the *Can-Can* is too absent-minded to realise what he is drinking."

"I never thought the French would be as foolish as that!" Valeria replied.

They were talking in very low voices.

The Master of Ceremonies in the centre of the dance-floor was explaining what a magnificent programme they had tonight to delight their patrons.

He gave the names of several performers.

When he mentioned Mimi Blanc, there was wild applause and several shouts of appreciation.

He then went on to introduce the three acrobats who were to open the Show.

They were obviously not of great interest to the audience.

Although the Band played loudly as they started to perform some spectacular stunts, everybody was talking.

Tony had not taken his eyes from the dance-floor for a moment.

He turned his head when the *Comte* said:

"I think we should introduce ourselves. I suspect you already heard my name. But I am naturally curious and I think, *Monsieur,* you are English, are you not?"

"Is it so obvious?" Tony asked. "But of course you are right, *Monsieur le Comte.* My name is Antony Archer."

"And *Madame*?" the *Comte* enquired.

Valeria was aware that he had already seen the rings on the third finger of her left hand.

It was why he addressed her as *"Madame."*

The *Comte* was looking at her, and she replied without waiting for Tony:

"My name is . . . Vala Hérard."

She was delighted with herself for remembering it so easily.

She thought Tony would be pleased with her.

Instead, however, he was looking at the young woman, who was little more than a girl, seated on his left.

"And *Mademoiselle*?" he enquired.

"Renée," she replied, "and I am sure it is a name you will not forget."

"How could I do that?" Tony asked gallantly.

She had dark hair, heavily mascaraed eye-lashes, and a small crimson mouth.

She was not strictly pretty, but she had a *gamin* charm which Valeria recognised as being peculiarly French.

She was also wearing a gown with a very low and revealing décolletage.

She wore no hat on her head, but some cleverly arranged osprey feathers fluttered when she moved.

The waiter, on the *Comte*'s instructions, had filled Valeria's glass as well as his.

As he turned to go away, Valeria said in a low voice to the *Comte*:

"Please do not let Tony drink anything that is bad for him."

The *Comte*'s lips twisted, and she thought that she must appear to be imposing on him.

Hastily she added:

"We will, of course, pay for it."

"On the contrary, *Madame*," the *Comte* replied, "as you are sitting at my table, you are my guests."

Valeria would have protested.

But she felt from the way he spoke that he was determined to have his own way.

She therefore answered:

"Thank you, thank you very much!"

The *Comte* then ordered another bottle of the special champagne.

The one which Tony had been given when they arrived was removed.

The acrobats finished their act and were replaced by a man with a Magic Lantern.

He showed extraordinary creatures, caricatures, and jokes in silhouette on a screen just by using his fingers and hands.

It was very cleverly done, but again the audience was talking.

The *Comte* said to Valeria:

"Tell me about yourself. I do not remember ever seeing you before."

"We arrived only two hours ago," Valeria replied.

"From Paris?" he questioned.

"No, from England," Valeria said, again without thinking.

"So that accounts for Mr. Archer," the *Comte* remarked.

She answered him more or less automatically, looking round the room as she did so.

She was thinking it strange that, after all their efforts to get there, nobody seemed interested in the performance that was taking place in front of them.

Now that she thought she had been indiscreet, she felt she must cover her tracks.

"We came by train," she said, "and it was a long journey."

"Then you might have found it more amusing to stay where you were, rather than come to this rumbustiousness."

Valeria remembered that was the word her Grandmother had used to describe *le chahut*.

Yet the *Moulin de la Mer* was not the vulgar, dirty place she had described; at any rate, not at the moment.

As if the *Comte* were following her thoughts, he said:

"Tonight it is very quiet and well-behaved compared to how it can be at times, but I am rather surprised, *Madame,* that you should visit something which is certainly essentially for *les hommes*."

Valeria looked away from him.

Then, realising that he expected an answer, she replied:

"Mr. Archer, being English, had heard so much about the *Can-Can* of the *Moulin Rouge*. As we were unable to go to Paris at the moment, he was delighted to find he could see it in Biarritz."

"It is certainly a good imitation," the *Comte* said in what sounded a lofty tone.

As they were talking, Valeria realised that Tony was whispering to *Mademoiselle* Renée.

She was obviously very amused by what he was saying to her.

She talked to him as the French invariably do, accentuating her words with her eyes, her lips, her hands, and even the movement of her shoulders.

The performance with the Magic Lantern came to an end, and there was some half-hearted applause.

Then the Master of Ceremonies who had spoken first came on to say in a tone of excitement:

"And now, *Messieurs et Mesdames*! The Star of the evening! The dancer for whom you have all been waiting—the toast of Paris, now the Queen of Biarritz—Mimi Blanc!"

There was enthusiastic applause and shouts from the back of the hall.

Looking behind her, Valeria realised there was a number of men who were apparently unable to find tables, drinking at the Bar.

Mimi Blanc came onto the floor and the applause was deafening.

She looked to Valeria to be about the same age as herself.

She had a strange, almost baby face which at the same time seemed to be debauched.

She had a mouth that seemed to stretch almost from ear to ear, and yet was tantalisingly provocative.

She had a milky-white bosom which appeared to be escaping from her *corsage*.

Every gesture she made seemed somehow to have a different meaning than what it would ordinarily have had.

Valeria naturally had no idea that the Producers of the entertainment in the *Moulin de la Mer* had searched the whole of France for such a dancer.

What they wanted was one who could command the same attention as Louise Weber, who was the Star of the *Moulin Rouge*.

"La Goulue," as she was known in Paris, was the most erotic dancer in Montmartre.

Her name meant "glutton," which came from her habit of greedily drinking the last dregs from a glass.

It also described her eternal search for sensual pleasure.

Louise had been a washer-girl and artist's model and a dancer from an early age.

A child of the streets, she had wandered from café to café, Dance Hall to Dance Hall.

It was her high kicks and animal vitality which had made her the Star of the *Moulin Rouge*.

She was as great a draw as the *Can-Can* itself.

Mimi Blanc was determined to out-dance and certainly out-do in every other particular the woman she had been told to copy.

As she came onto the dance-floor, as soon as she could make herself heard, she made some very lewd remarks.

They were in an *argot* which fortunately Valeria did not understand.

This was followed by a great roar of laughter which gradually died down when she began to dance.

It was dancing that did not resemble in any way what Valeria had ever seen before.

She did not understand that like *La Goulue*, Mimi provoked those watching her by a display of bare flesh.

It appeared with every protuberant swirl of her under-clothes.

It was to the legion of men sitting watching her breathlessly a crude invitation which was almost bestial.

At the same time, she aroused the imagination with every twist of her limbs and every swirl of her hips.

As the music grew louder and louder, Mimi's movements became quicker and quicker.

Valeria felt the blood rise to infuse her cheeks.

While she told herself it was foolish, she was, in fact, extremely shocked.

How was it possible that any woman could behave in a public place in what Valeria knew was the very depths of vulgarity?

She was, however, intelligent enough to know that because it was so unusual, because Mimi was so uninhibited, it appealed to everything that was animal in the men who watched her.

The music grew faster and faster and Mimi's dancing became more and more abandoned.

Valeria looked down at her hands, which were clasped together in her lap, and shut her eyes.

She did not see the climax of the dance when Mimi was going into an orgasmic ecstasy.

Panting and half-undressed, she collapsed onto the floor in the *grand écart*, with her legs stretched out horizontally.

Above Valeria's head she heard the wild applause which seemed about to take off the roof.

Only when Mimi Blanc had taken bow after bow, bending so low that her breasts showed very clearly, did she leave the floor.

Shouting something very lewd, she disappeared.

Valeria opened her eyes.

It was then she was aware that the *Comte* was looking not at Mimi but at her.

When it was obvious Mimi would not return, the applause died down.

Valeria drank a little of the champagne, aware as she did so that the water she had asked for had not materialised.

She was about to ask Tony if he would order it again, when there was a roll of drums.

76

A feeling of excitement went over the whole hall which told her the *Can-Can* was about to commence.

A second later the dancers were on the floor with their arms across each other's shoulders.

Their dresses swung with every movement of their legs.

Valeria knew then that Tony could neither hear nor see anything but what was happening in front of him.

The Band struck up a wild tune and the dancers began with a few simple steps.

They then started to work up to the same frenzy which had activated Mimi.

They spun round like tops, turned cartwheels, and punctuated their gyrations with the famous high kicks.

Valeria had to admire when, as she had expected, a dancer stood on the toes of one foot, holding her other as high as possible with one hand.

Then, after every girl had taken it in turns to do something spectacular, they all started to kick their legs in unison.

Every man in the room clapped his hands in time to the music and the rising movement of the dancers' legs.

The noise was deafening and the excitement infectious.

The girls' black stockings and frilly white knickers seemed to rise and fall until everyone watching was mesmerised by them.

Then, as they all subsided, their legs horizontal on the dance-floor, the applause, the shrieks, and yells of excitement as the men rose from their

77

seats, clapping vigorously, was a sight in itself.

Tony was, of course, on his feet with the others.

But the *Comte* sat back with a cynical expression on his face which made Valeria look at him in surprise.

Why, she wondered, did he come to such a place if he felt like that about it?

It was impossible to speak above the din.

Only when the dancers finally left the floor did the men sit down again at their tables.

The Band struck up a Waltz.

It was then, to Valeria's surprise, that Tony asked *Mademoiselle* Renée to dance.

She glanced at the *Comte,* as if seeking his permission.

When he gave a slight nod of his head she swept onto the floor and Tony's arm was around her waist.

Valeria watched them moving amongst the other couples until the *Comte* said:

"Do you wish to dance, *Madame?*"

"Thank you, but I would rather not."

"I agree with you, and this is not the right place for you."

She wondered what he meant.

At the same time, she had no wish to go onto the crowded floor.

She noticed that most of the men were dancing in a very intimate manner with their partners.

It would have offended her Father considerably if that had happened to her.

It struck her that it was bad manners on Tony's part to have taken away the *Comte*'s friend without asking his permission.

She therefore said in a tentative, slightly embarrassed manner:

"I hope . . . you do not . . . mind Tony . . . dancing with . . . your friend."

"If you do not mind, why should I?" the *Comte* replied. "And as it happens, she is not *my friend*."

He accentuated the words and when Valeria looked at him in surprise, he explained:

"When a man comes alone to the *Moulin* he is expected to give one of the 'hostesses,' which is a polite word for them, a drink."

Valeria looked towards the Bar, where she had seen a crowd of unaccompanied young women when she first arrived.

There were only a few left now.

When she looked around she saw that at practically every table there was a made-up woman not wearing a hat.

She supposed this proclaimed them to be what the *Comte* had called "hostesses."

She could think of nothing to say, so she just sat watching the dancers.

Finally Tony and Renée came back to the table.

Tony sat down next to Valeria and said in a low voice:

"Listen, Valeria, I do not suppose you want to stay and see the same Show over again, and I have been invited to a party. Would you mind if I took you back to the Hôtel and then returned here?"

Valeria was so surprised that for a moment she could not speak.

Then, before she could do so, the *Comte* who had obviously overheard what Tony had said, interrupted.

"As I am leaving, *Monsieur*," he said, "may I offer to escort *Madame* Hérard back to where you are staying? My carriage is outside, and there will be no difficulty in my dropping her wherever she wishes to go."

"That is very kind of you, *Monsieur le Comte*," Tony replied. "You are sure it will be no trouble?"

"No trouble at all," the *Comte* replied.

Tony looked at his sister.

"You will be all right," he said, "and it is only a short drive to the *Hôtel*."

Valeria wanted to expostulate and insist that he come with her.

She knew by the way Tony was looking at Renée that it must be her party to which he was going.

She therefore said:

"I . . . I am sure . . . I shall be . . . all right."

"Thanks, Vala, you are a sport!" Tony replied.

As he rose to take Renée back onto the dance-floor, the *Comte* got to his feet.

"Shall we go?" he asked. "I am sure you are finding it hot and rather uncomfortable in here."

Valeria picked up her wrap which she had lain across the back of her chair.

Because there were so many people crowding the room, the *Comte* went ahead of her to clear the way.

He was obviously well-known in the *Moulin*, for not only the *Maître d'Hôtel*, but also several waiters bowed as he walked towards the door.

Only as he got there did a waiter say:

"There's a large crowd outside, *Monsieur le Comte*."

The *Comte* stopped and said to Valeria:

"Wait here a moment while I find my carriage which is waiting for me."

Valeria was just inside the main doors.

She realised it had been closed to keep out those for whom there was no accommodation inside the hall.

The man opened it just a fraction to let the *Comte* out.

As he disappeared, a voice beside her said:

"*Madame,* I have been trying to attract your attention all evening!"

She looked round in surprise.

Standing behind her was a man who did not look French and was not particularly prepossessing.

At the same time, he was fairly young, dark, and correctly dressed.

When he spoke again she thought he must be Spanish.

"What I have to say to you," the man said in a low voice, "is that I will give you double—no, treble, if you like, of whatever you are receiving from that man. I want you to come away with me—now, at this moment!"

Valeria stared at him in sheer astonishment.

She did not understand what he was saying, and he repeated:

"I have never seen anybody so beautiful, and I am a rich man. Come—come now!"

"No . . . of course . . . not," Valeria replied.

He put out his hand to hold on to her.

With a little cry she ran towards the door through which the *Comte* had disappeared.

As she reached it he was coming back for her.

Because she was frightened, she put out her hand towards him, saying:

"Take me away from here . . . take me away . . . quickly!"

The *Comte* did not ask questions.

He saw by her expression that something had occurred to upset her.

Taking her by the arm, he drew her across the pavement into a carriage that was waiting.

A footman held open the door, and Valeria hurried inside, the *Comte* following her.

The footman did not, however, shut the door, but stood waiting for instructions.

"I do not know where you are staying," the *Comte* said, "but I suggest, as it is not very late, we might have a drink first, somewhere where it is quiet."

"You have already given me a drink," Valeria replied, "but if it is not too much trouble, I would like something to eat."

She was suddenly aware that she was, in fact, very hungry.

She had eaten nothing since she and Tony had a light luncheon in the yacht.

"Of course!" the *Comte* agreed. "And it is what I would like myself, having had no dinner."

He gave the order to the footman, who shut the door, and the horses started off.

As they did so, Valeria said:

"Perhaps it is . . . wrong for me to . . . ask you when . . . you have already been . . . so kind as to say that you will . . . take me home?"

"You may go home whenever you wish to," the *Comte* said, "but we are both hungry, so I will introduce you to a quiet place where the food is excellent and we can talk as we were unable to do in that noisy hall."

He had a deep voice and he was speaking in a quiet, controlled manner.

It made Valeria sure he was very different from the Spaniard who had just spoken to her.

Once again she gave a little shudder, and the *Comte* asked:

"What happened to frighten you while I was away?"

"A . . . a man . . . spoke to . . . me."

"That is surely what you might have expected in the *Moulin*?"

"How could I . . . expect anything like . . . that?" Valeria asked beneath her breath.

Then she told herself she had willingly gone to a place where there was a dancer like Mimi Blanc.

She must therefore expect men to treat her different from the way they would in an English Ballroom.

"What did he say to you?" the *Comte* asked.

"I . . . I cannot talk . . . about it," Valeria replied. "I was . . . just thinking that it was my own . . . fault for going . . . to a place like . . . that!"

"But your friend Tony persuaded you. Another time you must tell him to look after you better."

"Yes, of course," Valeria agreed. "But he is young and he has been longing to go to Paris. But my Fa—his Father would not . . . let him."

She had very nearly said "my Father," and she told herself she must be much more careful.

They had driven only a short distance before the carriage came to a standstill.

They had stopped outside a small Restaurant

which looked quiet and respectable.

She had never dined in a Restaurant and never, of course, been alone with a man.

When she had been with her Mother in Normandy she had seen small Restaurants in the streets when they were out shopping.

She had wondered at the time what they were like inside.

The *Comte,* who was obviously well-known, was led to the far end of the room, where there was a table in front of a curved sofa.

The ends of it acted like a screen.

Those seated on the sofa could not be seen clearly by the other diners.

There were, in fact, only two more sofa tables and half-a-dozen round ones in the whole place.

There were pictures on the wall which Valeria thought had been executed by local artists.

They were doubtless for sale.

The tables were elegantly laid with small vases of flowers, and there was a lighted candle on each one.

There were only about six other diners in the place.

As Valeria sat down she thought how quiet and peaceful it was compared to the noise, smoke, and excitable atmosphere at the *Moulin.*

"Shall I order what I think you would like?" the *Comte* asked.

"Yes, please," Valeria answered.

The *Comte* ordered the meal, then studied the wine-list.

"Would you like to drink champagne?" he enquired.

"Please," Valeria replied, "I do not want to drink very much, but I am thirsty. I asked Tony to order me some mineral water at the *Moulin,* but it never came."

"Of course not," the *Comte* said as he smiled. "If you are thirsty, you must drink their champagne, which is very expensive! They are far too sensible to quench your thirst with anything else!"

Valeria laughed.

"I never thought of that! But of course it is another clever way of making money!"

The *Comte* ordered some mineral water which was brought immediately.

As she sipped it, Valeria said:

"Thank you, and although it is something I should not do, I am very excited to see inside a Restaurant, and how prettily it is decorated!"

"Something you should not do?"

Valeria thought quickly that she had made a gaffe and said:

"Of course it is . . . wrong of me to . . . accept dinner from a . . . Gentleman I have only just . . . met and to whom I have not . . . been formally . . . introduced."

The *Comte* smiled as if he knew she had intended something very different.

"I assure you, *Madame,*" he said, "you are doing me a great favour. I am delighted not to have to dine alone."

"You were not intending to take *Mademoiselle* Renée out to dinner?"

He shook his head.

"If you are interested, I was to dine with a Diplomat friend who unfortunately was called away just before I arrived. He left me a note expressing his regrets. Because I therefore had nowhere else to go, I went to the *Moulin*."

"But you had reserved a table," Valeria said.

The *Comte* smiled.

"I had actually reserved the table for the second Show, but because they knew me at the *Moulin* they were prepared to turn away a client who was of no particular importance!"

"Oh, I am so glad you let Tony stay!" Valeria said. "I think it would have broken his heart if he had not been able to see the *Can-Can* after all the fuss we have had in getting here!"

"Well, he had seen the *Can-Can*," the *Comte* said, "and now, apparently, he is going to a party."

He spoke in such a strange way that Valeria asked:

"You do not think there is anything . . . wrong about the party? It would not be illegal . . . or anything like that?"

She spoke in such an agitated way that the *Comte* replied soothingly:

"No, no, of course not. It only surprises me that you are not jealous that he wishes to be with the attractive *Mademoiselle* Renée."

"Jealous?" Valeria questioned without thinking.

Then, as if she understood what the *Comte* meant, she added:

"No, of course not! I have known Tony for many years, and we are very good friends."

She thought the *Comte* raised his eye-brows.

Then, as she thought it a mistake to pursue the subject, Valeria asked:

"Tell me about these pictures. Are there many

modern artists in Biarritz?"

"Like Paris, they have the so-called 'Impressionists,' " the *Comte* replied. "In fact, although perhaps
I should not admit it, I have bought one or two
myself."

"I would love to see them!" Valeria exclaimed. "I
have read so much about the Impressionists. I am
sure anything new is always disparaged and looked
down on by the older generations. But perhaps one
day they will become fashionable."

"Maybe," the *Comte* said doubtfully. "At the same
time, they have a new technique which I find interesting and is certainly different from that of the
acknowledged Masters."

"Do you collect pictures?" Valeria asked.

"I have a number of which I am very proud," the
Comte replied, "and I would like one day, as you
suggest, to show them to you."

"I would love to see them," Valeria replied.

Then she told herself that it was extremely
unlikely that she would ever see the *Comte* again.

It would be therefore a mistake to make appoint-
ments she could never keep.

"Are you thinking that what I have suggested is
impossible?" the *Comte* asked.

"How did you know that was what I was thinking?"

"I am reading your thoughts."

"That is ... something you should ... not do!"
Valeria objected.

"Why not?"

"Because my thoughts are my own and it would
frighten me if I thought you, or anybody else, could
guess what I am thinking."

"And are your thoughts really so bad?"

"No, of course . . . not, but they are . . . private, and they are . . . mine and mine . . . alone!"

"We shall see," the *Comte* answered, "and now tell me why you were so shocked at the dancing of Mimi Blanc."

Valeria stiffened.

"I . . . I do not want . . . to talk about . . . it."

"But you *were* shocked."

"Yes . . . I was. The *Can-Can* was very much as I . . . expected it to be . . . but I never . . . thought it . . . possible to see a woman dancing . . . in such an . . . indecent manner."

"How old are you?" the *Comte* asked.

Valeria drew in her breath.

She had been carried away by her denunciation of Mimi Blanc's act.

Now she felt she was on dangerous ground.

She had not discussed with Tony what she should say if anybody asked her her age.

She had never imagined it might happen.

She had no idea how old she should be.

Yet she was sure she looked very much older as she was than if she had been dressed like a *débutante*.

The *Comte* was waiting.

She had the idea that he was used to getting his own way, and being told the truth.

With an effort she said:

"I . . . I have always . . . understood that it is considered . . . rude for . . . a gentleman to ask . . . a lady's age, particularly if she is French."

"I stand rebuked!" the *Comte* replied.

"No . . . please," Valeria said, "I did not . . . mean

it like that ... and of course ... I want to be ... young. Everybody wants to be ... young."

"I think," the *Comte* said slowly, "you *are* young, and I am finding it irresistible not to guess your age and a great deal more, *Madame* Hérard, about you."

"I think that would be a mistake," Valeria said.

"A mistake?" he questioned.

"We have met tonight for the first time," she said, "and perhaps the last. We are 'ships that pass in the night.' Tomorrow I want to think this was just an exciting experience."

"But not one you would wish to occur again!"

"It is not a question of wishing," Valeria said. "I think it is something that will *not* occur again. Therefore I want to enjoy every minute and not feel guilty or embarrassed."

The *Comte* laughed.

"You may be very young in years, but you are certainly experienced in being devious and very provocative. I accept your challenge, *Madame* Hérard, because it is something I find extremely fascinating!"

"My ... challenge?" Valeria asked.

"To discover about you what you do not wish me to know, and shall I say I will find it very humiliating if you succeed in bewildering and amazing me and then you disappear, so I can never find you again."

Valeria thought with a smile that was exactly what would happen.

"Very well, *Monsieur le Comte*," she said, "it is a challenge, and I think it only fair to warn you it is one you will lose!"

chapter five

"THAT was a delicious dinner!" Valeria exclaimed as her plate was taken away from her.

"I am glad you enjoyed it," the *Comte* said. "I always think this is one of the best places in Biarritz, although it is not so popular as some of the larger Restaurants."

"I am fascinated by Biarritz," Valeria said, "and I have been reading its history."

"I thought you would," the *Comte* replied. "It surprises me, however, that you should be so well-read and intelligent, considering the life you lead."

Valeria was not certain what he meant by that, and she replied:

"I think now I should go home. I am sure Tony will worry if he comes back and finds I am not there."

"I doubt if he will return before the early hours,"

the *Comte* said dryly. "But of course, if that is what you wish, I will take you back to the Hôtel."

He sent for the bill which, Valeria noticed, he signed; then they left the Restaurant.

She wondered if he lived in Biarritz, but thought it was a mistake to ask personal questions.

Instead, as they drove away towards the Hôtel, she said:

"There is one thing I must see while I am in Biarritz, and that is the foam from the breakers. I believe they are always there whatever the weather."

"That is true," the *Comte* said, "and it is a very beautiful sight. I will take you to see them tomorrow."

Valeria gave him a quick glance.

"Tomorrow?" she questioned.

"I am asking you to have luncheon with me," the *Comte* answered, "then I will take you to see the waves, which are even more spectacular and far more beautiful for you to watch than the *Can-Can*."

Valeria felt there was almost a reproof in the comparison, and she said quickly:

"I am not sure what . . . Tony and I will be . . . doing tomorrow."

"Your friend is naturally included in the invitation," the *Comte* said, "but I have the feeling he will be otherwise engaged."

Valeria looked at him in surprise.

Then, because she had only just thought of it, she said:

"Perhaps his . . . friends who were giving . . . the party will ask him to be . . . with them."

"In which case, I hope you will be with me."

"It is very kind of you to invite me," Valeria answered, "but surely you have many engagements already?"

"As I mentioned earlier in the evening," the *Comte* replied, "I came to Biarritz to see my Diplomatic friend, as we had a number of things to discuss. Now that he has deserted me, I am on my own, and I can only beg you to take pity on me."

Valeria laughed.

"That sounds very plausible, but I am sure you have many friends in the Town who would be delighted to see you."

"Only if you refuse me," the *Comte* insisted.

As he spoke, the horses drew up outside the Hôtel.

"So this is where you are staying!" the *Comte* said. "I believe it is quite comfortable and quiet."

"That is what I thought," Valeria agreed, "although I had only a few minutes in which to change before Tony was anxious to hurry to the *Moulin de la Mer* in case it was too late to get a table."

She paused before she added:

"I must thank you again for being so kind and not having us sent away ignominiously to stand at the back of the hall."

"The moment I saw you," the *Comte* replied, "I knew it would be a mistake to send you away from me."

Valeria's eyes widened.

Then, as the footman opened the door of the carriage, there was no need for her to answer, and she got out.

The *Comte* followed her, and as they stood out-side the front-door, he said:

"You are quite certain you will be all right? You are not frightened at being alone until your friend returns?"

"I am . . . sure I will . . . be all . . . right," Valeria answered.

At the same time, it struck her it was rather frightening to be alone in a strange Hôtel.

As if he read her thoughts, the *Comte* said:

"I know what I will do. Tell me where your room is, and I will walk into the garden. If you wave to me from the window, I shall know you are safe."

"There is . . . really no need . . ." Valeria began.

Then she thought it would at least be reassuring if that was what he did.

She had a sudden frightened feeling that some-thing might have gone wrong in the Hôtel.

Perhaps their rooms had been changed or, like the table, promised to somebody else.

"Your room looks on to the garden?" the *Comte* asked.

"Yes, I can see the fountain from my window."

"Then that is where I shall wait," he answered.

She smiled at him and held out her hand.

She had not put on her gloves since she had left the Restaurant.

As he took her hand in his, she felt the strength of his fingers.

There was also what she thought was a vibration which seemed to pass from his hand to hers.

He bent his head and, raising her hand to his lips, to her surprise actually kissed it.

She felt his lips against her skin.

Because it made her shy, she took her hand away and slipped through the door into the entrance-hall.

There was only a sleepy Porter on duty behind the desk.

She asked for her key, and he handed it to her.

Then she ran up the stairs to the First Floor.

When she reached it, she was not certain in which direction her room lay.

Then she found it, and opening the door of her bedroom, went inside.

There was an oil-lamp left burning on the dressing-table, and she could see her belongings scattered about.

The door was open into the Sitting-Room, which was in darkness, but beyond it Tony's door was open.

There was also an oil-lamp burning there.

She could see the bed was unoccupied and knew he had not returned.

She put down her wrap, went to the window, and opened it.

Outside there was the balcony which she had noticed when she first arrived.

She stepped onto it and looked down into the garden.

The small fountain was still playing, and standing in front of it was the *Comte*.

He looked tall, strong, and reassuring.

She felt as if she were seeing him for the first time.

He was in some way different from how she had thought of him when he had first sat beside her at the *Moulin*.

She leaned over the balcony and waved her hand. He raised his in response.

Then, because she thought anyone watching would think it too intimate, she waved again and went back into her bedroom.

She imagined he would immediately walk away and drive back in his carriage.

"He has been very kind," she told herself.

She knew if she had come back with Tony, he would just have dropped her off and driven away again.

She would have been too nervous to order any food and would have gone to bed hungry.

As she undressed she found herself hoping Tony would agree to them both having luncheon with the *Comte* tomorrow.

* * *

Valeria awoke at what was for her quite a late hour in the morning.

She realised as she did so that she had not heard Tony come in.

She had, in fact, lain awake for quite a long time, expecting to hear him return and longing to be told about the party.

Now the sun was streaming between the curtains.

She got out of bed to look out into the garden.

She almost expected to find the *Comte* as she had last seen him silhouetted against the fountain.

Then she told herself she was sure by this time he was regretting he had asked her and Tony to luncheon.

She had left the door into the Sitting-Room ajar the night before so that she could hear Tony return.

Now, as she went into the room, she saw his door was closed.

That meant he would be asleep.

Even as a small boy he had slept late in the morning.

When he was on his holidays from School her mother always said:

"Let him sleep. It is a good thing for him to break the habit of being up very early as they are at School. I want his holiday to be a restful as well as an exciting one."

"I must not wake Tony," Valeria said to herself now.

At the same time, she was impatient because she had so much to talk to him about.

She rang the bell.

When the waiter came, she ordered herself a French breakfast of hot *croissants*, coffee, and fruit.

The waiter also brought her a dish of *fraises des bois* which she enjoyed enormously.

She thought the last time she had enjoyed them in France she had been with her Mother.

She only hoped that in Heaven her Mother was not aware that she had seen last night the appalling dance performed by Mimi Blanc.

'Mama would have been very shocked!'

She told herself once again that none of their relations must ever know that she had been to the *Moulin de la Mer*.

They would not only be angry with her, but extremely angry with Tony for taking her there.

'He must be very careful,' she thought.

At that moment his door opened and Tony looked into the Sitting-Room.

"I thought I heard someone moving about in here," he said.

"Did the waiter wake you bringing my breakfast?" Valeria asked. "I am sorry. Were you very late?"

"It is more truthful to say very early," Tony answered.

He went back to his bedroom, then returned wearing a long dressing-gown.

It was frogged across the chest like the one her Father wore.

It made him look very military.

"What time did you come in?" Valeria asked.

"God knows!" Tony replied. "All I can tell you is that dawn had broken and there were no stars in the sky!"

Valeria laughed.

"It must have been a very good party!"

"Party?" Tony asked. "Oh—yes—very good!"

He did not seem to want to talk about it but ordered his breakfast.

It took some time in coming because he wanted something more substantial than *croissants*.

While he was waiting he sat down in an armchair by the window and said:

"Did the *Comte* bring you home safely?"

"Yes, of course," Valeria replied, "but he gave me something to eat first, as I was so hungry."

"Oh, Lord! I forgot about that!" Tony exclaimed. "But I doubt if you would have got anything at the *Moulin*."

"If I had, I expect it would have been like the

champagne," Valeria replied.

Tony did not answer, and she went on:

"The *Comte* has asked us to luncheon today, and I would like to go, as he has promised to show us the breakers on the *Côte des Basques*. As I told you, I read about them in one of the books on the yacht."

"He has asked us to luncheon?" Tony repeated.

"He has certainly been very kind," Valeria replied. "He gave me a most delicious dinner last night in a small Restaurant which was exactly what I expected a French Restaurant to look like."

"He certainly seems a decent sort of fellow!" Tony agreed.

He paused. Then he asked:

"Would you mind very much having luncheon alone with him? I told Renée we would take her out, but three is always an awkward number."

Valeria stared at him in astonishment. Then she said:

"I . . . understood from the *Comte* that Renée is . . . one of what they call . . . 'hostesses' at the *Moulin*."

"Yes, she is," Tony agreed, "and she is a very attractive girl."

He got up from the table and walked to the window.

With his back to his sister, he said:

"I know it would be a mistake for you to associate with Renée, but quite frankly, Vala, I want to see her. She has told me the most interesting things about the Show and the *Can-Can*. Incidentally, I am going to meet all the dancers tonight."

"Another party?" Valeria asked.

"Yes—of course," Tony agreed. "Another party."

He spoke rather quickly, as if he were hiding something, but Valeria only said in a small voice:

"Then . . . what do . . . you want . . . me to do?"

Tony turned from the window.

"Look, Vala," he said, "I know I am behaving badly over this, but you do see—it is my only chance to enjoy myself as I have wanted to do for a long time."

He drew in his breath.

"Tomorrow we go to stay with all those French relations of yours, who will be extremely stuffy if I know anything about it. After that it will be home again, to be tied once more to Papa's apron-strings, as if I were a small child."

He spoke bitterly, and because Valeria loved him, she said:

"Of course, dearest, I understand. I will have luncheon with the *Comte,* and if by any lucky chance he asks me to dinner, I shall accept. Otherwise I will stay here on my own."

"You could go back to the yacht, although I told the Captain we were staying with friends in Biarritz," Tony said, "and he might think it a bit strange."

"No, I shall be all right," Valeria replied, "but there is one thing you must promise me."

"What is that?" Tony asked.

"That you will never, never, let anyone know what we have been doing. Papa would be furious and Mama would not have approved of me being at the *Moulin de la Mer.*"

"I realised that last night, when I watched Mimi Blanc," Tony agreed. "Of course she is quite fantastic, and Renée tells me that no one has ever danced like that except for *La Goulue* in Paris, whom she has copied."

"Then you do understand that I do not want to go to the *Moulin* tonight," Valeria said.

"If you are quite sure you will be all right," Tony said.

Then he said:

"I know I am behaving badly . . ."

He spoke so disarmingly that Valeria could only laugh.

Even as a small boy Tony had always admitted when he was in the wrong, and said he was sorry.

It was a very endearing part of his character.

"Enjoy yourself," she said. "I agree that is what you should do, and I promise you I can look after myself."

Tony looked relieved, then he said:

"For a Frenchman the *Comte* seems a gentleman, if that is the right word. I hope he did not make any advances to you last night?"

"No, of course he did not!" Valeria said. "He just brought me home and asked us both to have luncheon with him today."

She thought for a moment before she said:

"He did not say he would call for us, but I will be ready at about twelve-thirty."

"In which case I will make myself scarce before that!" Tony said. "There is no point in my going into details about what I shall be doing."

"No, of course not," Valeria agreed.

At the same time, she wondered what that actually implied.

She put on the most attractive of her cousin Gwendolyn's day-gowns.

She thought if she was truthful, she would really rather see the breakers with the *Comte* than with Tony.

He had always said that if there was anything that really bored him, it was sight-seeing.

It would make her uncomfortable if he was fidgetting about while the *Comte* was explaining things to her.

Tony, who had dressed more quickly, came into her room looking very dashing.

He was extremely good-looking in an English manner with fair hair, blue eyes, and well-cut features.

"I am off now," he said as Valeria turned round from the dressing-table.

She was applying, very carefully, a faint touch of rouge to her cheeks.

She had already put a minute amount of mascara to her eye-lashes.

"Do I look all right?" she asked Tony.

He looked at her critically before he said:

"I suppose there is nothing you can do about it, but you do look very young, and without the red lips, undoubtedly a Lady."

"Perhaps the *Comte* will not notice," Valeria replied. "And after all, he would hardly expect to find a Lady in the *Moulin de la Mer!*"

"That is true," Tony agreed. "Well, goodbye, Vala. You are being marvellous, as you know, and I really am grateful!"

He kissed her lightly on the cheek and went out of the room, shutting the door noisily behind him.

She heard his footsteps hurrying down the stairs and thought he was like a small boy being let out of School.

'He is happy, at any rate, Mama,' she said in her heart. 'I cannot believe he will get into any real trouble before we leave tomorrow."

She made her lips red and put on the very *chic* hat which went with the gown she was wearing.

It certainly, she thought, made her look older.

She slipped the ring onto her finger.

She was quite certain that no one would suspect for a moment that she had recently made her curtsy at Buckingham Palace.

When she was ready she went into the Sitting-Room to stand at the window, looking out at the fountain.

Suppose, after all, the *Comte* did not fetch her?

As she had suggested to him, they were "ships that pass in the night" and she might never see him again.

'I do want to see him again,' she thought. 'I do want to!'

Almost as if her wish were granted, the door of the Sitting-Room opened.

The servant who stood there announced:

"*Monsieur le Comte* de Savin, *Madame*!"

Valeria turned round.

The *Comte* was walking into the Sitting-Room and looking, she thought, even more attractive than he had last night.

"*Bonjour, Madame* Hérard!" he said as he reached her.

He raised her hand perfunctorily to his lips, but he did not kiss it.

"I was just . . . wondering," Valeria said a little breathlessly, "if you . . . really . . . wanted me to have . . . luncheon with . . . you."

"I asked you to do so, and I shall be very disappointed if you refuse," the *Comte* said.

"Then I am delighted to accept, but my . . . T-Tony thanks you very much for the i-invitation. He has h-however some . . . f-friends he particularly . . . w-wants to . . . s-see."

She stammered a little as she spoke.

She knew by the expression on the *Comte's* face that it was what he had expected.

"Then if you are ready," he said, "my horses are waiting, and I am taking you to what I think is a pleasant place which I hope you will enjoy."

"I am sure I shall," Valeria said, "and you have not forgotten what I wanted to see?"

"The *Côte des Basques*—I remember everything you said to me," the *Comte* said simply, "and perhaps I should tell you that you look very beautiful this morning, in fact, although it seems impossible, even lovelier than you were last night."

Because they were speaking in French, Valeria had not expected to be in any way embarrassed by the compliment.

She had had so many of them in England that they had ceased to make her shy.

Now, unaccountably, she felt the colour rising in her cheeks, and her eye-lashes flickered.

"Many men must have told you the same thing," the *Comte* remarked almost harshly. "It is therefore something you must be bored with hearing."

"Could anyone be bored with hearing nice things about one's self?" Valeria asked. "It is the unkind and untrue ones that hurt."

"I cannot believe," he said, "that you have ever been hurt in such a way, but, of course, you are deliberately mysterious about yourself."

"Think how dull it would be if I were just an 'open book,' and nothing came as a surprise," Valeria replied.

The *Comte* laughed.

"You are quite safe. You have surprised me from the very first moment I saw you, and I have continued to be surprised every moment since."

"Then at least you will not be yawning before we have finished luncheon," Valeria flashed.

"Come along," he said. "I promise to tell you when I am bored, and there will be no need for you to say anything—I shall read it in your eyes."

"If you are going to continue to read my thoughts as you did last night," Valeria replied, "I shall wear a pair of coloured spectacles!"

"That would be like deliberately shutting out the sun!" the *Comte* answered.

He opened the Sitting-Room door as he spoke, and Valeria walked out into the corridor.

She thought as they went down the stairs that it was very stimulating to be with him.

In some way she could not explain, he forced her to think more quickly than anyone had ever done before.

It was something she knew was happening while they were at luncheon.

She felt almost as if they were actors in a Play.

They were speaking lines that were witty and amusing and she imagined they had been written for them by one of the great Masters of Drama.

The Restaurant to which the *Comte* took her was certainly dramatic.

It was high above the *Grand Plage*.

They sat in a bow window from which they could see the golden sand and the sea—a deep blue in the sunshine.

Again it was a small Restaurant and the food which the *Comte* ordered was delicious.

He insisted on Valeria drinking a very fine and, she was sure, very expensive white wine.

It was amusing to realise that if she had been herself, she would not have been expected to drink wine at luncheon or dinner.

At home the Butler filled her glass with lemonade without asking her if she required something different.

At the dinner-parties in London the servants invariably said:

"Lemonade, M'Lady?"

It would have been a very daring girl who would have replied that she wanted something stronger.

Valeria sipped her wine, but was careful not to drink more than one glass.

As if the *Comte* knew exactly what she wanted, he provided plenty of mineral water.

Afterwards she found it difficult to remember what they had discussed because there had been so many subjects.

Fortunately they were all things in which she was interested.

Finally the *Comte* asked;

"What do you enjoy doing more than anything else?"

She had a feeling he was expecting a somewhat

different answer from the one she gave.

"Riding!" she said. "I would rather ride than do anything else in the world!"

"That is something I did not expect!" the *Comte* exclaimed. "Where do you ride?"

"Wherever I am, and, of course, I ask for the very best horses and the most spirited ones."

She was thinking, as she spoke, of Crusader.

"I am sure that is not a difficult request," the *Comte* said. "And does your friend Tony possess some fine horses?"

Just for a moment Valeria did not understand what the *Comte* was implying.

Then she said quickly:

"I have a horse of my own which is superior to any other animal I have ever seen, and I have had him since he was a Yearling. Because I love him, he responds to everything I ask of him."

"Just as any man you loved would do the same," the *Comte* remarked.

"I doubt it!" Valeria replied. "Men are usually thinking about themselves. Crusader thinks about me, just as I think about him."

"So you prefer horses to diamonds," the *Comte* remarked, "but you expect them both."

Valeria looked at him with a puzzled expression on her face.

Then she remembered that last night she had been wearing her mother's necklace.

Of course the *Comte* would think that as she had been married, her husband would have given them to her.

Again he must have been reading her thoughts, for he said:

"Tell me about your husband. You never mention him. Did you love him very deeply?"

Valeria felt suddenly as if a pit had opened up in the ground beneath her feet.

She was on dangerous ground, and she turned her face towards the window.

"Because everything here is new and exciting," she said, "I have no wish to talk of what is past."

"So you were not happy," the *Comte* said quietly.

"Someone once said to me," Valeria replied, "never think about yesterday, but enjoy today because there may be no tomorrow."

"An easy philosophy," the *Comte* said simply, "for those who do not have many days left!"

Valeria laughed.

"You always have an answer for everything," she said, "and I do so enjoy being with you!"

"And I enjoy being with you," the *Comte* said, "so much that I am afraid."

"Afraid? Of what?"

"That I shall lose you."

Valeria shrugged her shoulders in what she knew was a typically French fashion.

"That is inevitable," she said, "and that is why today is important."

"If only you really meant that," the *Comte* said.

"Of course I mean it! Today is very important to me because I am having such a lovely time, and I do not want anything to spoil it."

"Then I must make sure that nothing does!" the *Comte* answered.

They left the Restaurant and found the carriage waiting to drive them along the *Grand Plage*.

Then they walked along the Promenade towards the sea.

What fascinated Valeria was that everywhere there were great bushes of Hydrangeas.

Pink, crimson, and blue, they opened in the niches in the rocks, filling every available space.

It made, she thought, Biarritz a City of Blossom.

When they reached the place where they could see the breakers foaming in towards the shore, Valeria was entranced.

"I am sure it is different from anywhere else in the world," she said, "and this is really Fairyland with its flowers, its golden sands, and magical sea!"

Then she was aware that while she was looking down at the breakers, the *Comte* was looking only at her.

There was an expression in his eyes that made her feel a little quiver move within her.

She did not understand what it was.

It was a sensation she had never had before, and certainly not with any of the men with whom she had danced in London.

She sat down on a seat surrounded by Hydrangeas.

She felt that nothing could be more romantic.

Once again it was as if they were on a stage.

The lines, witty and alive, seemed to come from their lips without their thinking about them.

As the *Comte* laughed and laughed again she told herself that her Mother would have been proud of her.

When Valeria was about fifteen her Mother had said to her:

"If you have entertained the man you are with, dearest, you will hold his interest."

"But how does one know what will interest him, Mama!" Valeria had asked.

"When in doubt," her Mother had said, "ask a man about himself. There is no subject he finds more interesting!"

They had both laughed.

It was something Valeria had remembered.

She had found when her dinner-partner was an elderly man she had only to ask him about himself for the conversation to flow without any difficulty.

Yet, if she was being elusive, so was the *Comte*.

She tried time after time to entice him into saying something revealing.

He always managed to remain an enigma, just as she did.

'He is paying me out in my own coin!' she thought.

Only when he was driving her back to the Hôtel did he ask:

"What are your plans for this evening?"

He had not asked her before.

She had been half-afraid that he would say good-bye, and that would be the end.

She hesitated a moment before she replied:

"I . . . hardly like to . . . tell . . . you."

"I wonder if I am right in thinking that your friend Tony is going to another party this evening?"

"How did you guess?" Valeria exclaimed. "He is going to meet the *Can-Can* girls, and as you can imagine, he would rather do that than anything else in the world!"

"That I *cannot* imagine," the *Comte* replied, "because I would rather be with you."

Valeria waited, and he said:

"Will you therefore do me the honour of dining with me?"

She laughed before she said:

"I was so afraid you would not ask me, and I am sure the food at the Hôtel is not very good."

"I promise you a delicious dinner," the *Comte* said. "Shall we dine early?"

"It may sound very un-French," Valeria said, "but I have grown used to English hours."

"Which is, of course, what Mr. Archer would enjoy!" the *Comte* remarked.

There was silence, then he said:

"I will collect you at a quarter-to-eight."

"You are quite sure you really want me?" Valeria asked. "I feel I am . . . foisting myself upon you . . . but I never . . . expected Tony would find . . . friends in Biarritz and leave me on . . . my own."

"That is certainly something that will not happen," the *Comte* said, "and I shall look forward to renewing our duel with words, and will polish up my foil!"

She knew he was referring to his tongue, and she laughed before she said:

"Now you are frightening me, and if I am vanquished in the first few minutes, it will be very humiliating."

"I think that is unlikely," the *Comte* said, "and there are a large number of subjects we have not yet explored."

He paused before he added:

"Love being the most obvious!"

"I think that is barred," Valeria said quickly.

"Why?" the Comte enquired.

"Because it is unfair. I am sure you know far more about it than I do, and I should therefore start with a large handicap."

She thought, as she spoke, that she had been clever.

But the *Comte* said:

"If that is true, then it is another challenge to which I am determined to find the answer."

The horses stopped outside the Hôtel, and when Valeria had got out, she held out her hand.

"Thank you, thank you so very much!" she said. "It has been a very exciting day so far, and I am looking forward to the evening."

"I, too, far more than I can say," he replied.

He spoke with a sincerity which was somehow surprising.

She had grown used to the touch of sarcasm in his voice.

Sometimes there was an undoubtedly mocking note which made her feel nervous.

He kissed her hand, and just for a second his lips brushed her skin.

What startled her was that as he did so she felt as if a streak of lightning ran through her body.

It was so intense that it was almost painful.

Yet when it was gone she thought she must have imagined it.

At the same time, because it was so strange, she hurried away from him to collect her key from the man at the desk.

This time she was given the key to the Sitting-Room.

As she walked into it she was astonished at what she saw.

There were flowers—flowers she had not expected and which she thought must have been given to her by the *Comte*.

There was an enormous arrangement of pink and white roses that was very beautiful.

A card was attached to them.

Written in what she had expected would be a strong and upright hand, she read:

Thank you for the most delightful evening I have ever spent.

Ramon de Savin.

'So that is his name!' Valeria thought. 'And Ramon suits him.'

She felt it was strong and very masculine.

Then she turned to the other flowers which were almost as spectacular as the roses.

It was a basket of orchids which was obviously a very expensive gift.

She picked up the card, thinking it strange that the *Comte* should send her two presents.

Written in French were the words:

To the most beautiful woman I have ever seen!

Luis Gonzalaz.

For a moment she just stared at the signature.

Then she realised it must be the Spaniard who had spoken to her last night.

She wondered how he had found out who she was and where she was staying.

It was something she certainly would not have wished him to know.

Then she told herself he could have found out from *Mademoiselle* Renée.

If he had questioned her and she was an employee at the *Moulin,* she would feel obliged to tell him the truth.

Valeria flung the Spaniard's card down on the table.

For a moment she felt a little afraid.

Then she remembered that tomorrow she and Tony would be going away.

Then neither the Spaniard nor anybody else they had met here would find them again.

That also included the *Comte.*

Something within her cried out because, although she did not want to admit it, she had no wish to lose him.

chapter six

"IT has been a wonderful day!" Valeria said as the *Comte* drove her back after dinner.

"Do you mean that?" he enquired.

"Of course I mean it!" she said. "I cannot remember ever having enjoyed myself so much!"

It was not only the beauty of the things the *Comte* had shown her.

Never before had she been with a man whom she found so interesting.

They had discussed a dozen different topics last night.

Yet today they found there was hardly a subject in the world about which they had not argued, and sometimes agreed.

The only person in the past that she had been able to talk to so easily had been her Father.

He was, however, rather dictatorial and so intent

upon putting forth his own point of view that he hardly listened to hers.

It was a compliment in itself that the *Comte* listened and did not disparage or belittle anything she said.

'If this is being alone with a man,' she thought as they drove along, 'then it is much more enjoyable than I ever realised it could be.'

The *Comte,* who had been silent, suddenly said:

"There is something different about which I want to talk to you, Vala."

There was a more serious note in his voice than there had been before.

Instinctively she knew that he was going to talk about themselves, and it was something she could not permit.

Before she could think of what to say, he went on:

"I think you know already what I feel about you, and therefore—"

Valeria held up her hand.

"Stop!" she said. "You will spoil . . . everything if you . . . drive away the . . . dreamlike feeling I have had all day!"

"It has also been dreamlike for me," the *Comte* replied.

"If we talk about it, it will vanish," she said. "Dreams are like Fairy gold and must not be touched by human hands . . . so I will . . . not listen."

She put her hands over her ears as she spoke, and as she did so looked through the window.

She realised they were not far from the Hôtel.

There was no time for him to say what he wanted to.

Something within her cried out at the thought

that she would never see the *Comte* again.

But she knew it would be wrong to raise his hopes or allow him to say anything he would regret later.

She moved her fingers from her ears and the *Comte* said:

"I have no wish to spoil the perfection of our time together. Have luncheon with me again tomorrow. I am sure I can find other things to show you, and of course other things to talk to you about."

Valeria drew in her breath.

She wondered if she should be honest and tell him that tomorrow she would not be here.

Then she asked herself what was the point?

It would spoil the wonder and joy she felt and which she thought in a small way he felt too because they were together.

And if she did tell him she was going away, how could she explain why?

He must never guess she was not what she appeared to be.

It was actually with a sense of relief that she realised the horses were drawing up outside the Hôtel.

As he had done last night, the *Comte* escorted her to the front-door.

Then, as she looked up at him, he said:

"I will call for you at twelve-thirty, as I did today, and thank you for what you called a 'dreamlike' day."

"It is something I shall always remember," Valeria said.

"So shall I," the *Comte* answered.

They stood looking at each other.

Valeria felt they were saying things in their hearts which had nothing to do with the movement of their lips.

Then she put out her hand.

The *Comte* took it in his and kissed it, and again she felt the touch of his lips on her skin.

Lightning shot through her, and as it did so he turned her hand over and kissed the palm.

It was something which had never happened before.

Now there was an even more violent response within her.

It frightened her, and she took her hand away to push open the door.

"I will wait by the fountain," the *Comte* said, "until I know you are safe."

Valeria smiled at him.

Then, because she was afraid of her feelings, she hurried into the Hôtel.

The Porter automatically handed her the key of her room, and without speaking she ran up the stairs.

"I am . . . leaving him . . . how can . . . I leave . . . him?" she was asking.

She knew it was the hardest thing she had ever had to do in her whole life—to say goodbye without telling him she would never see him again.

The Porter had given her the key to her bedroom, and she unlocked the door.

To her surprise, the oil-lamp had not been lit.

The curtains, however, were drawn back and the window was open onto the balcony.

She had pulled off her hat as she had come up the stairs.

Now she flung it down on the bed and walked towards the window.

As she did so, something large, dark, and very frightening came from the shadows in the corner of the room.

Valeria stopped dead.

Then, as she realised who it was, she screamed and screamed again.

*　*　*

The *Comte* walked slowly from the front-door across the grass.

Turning the corner of the Hôtel, he moved into the garden.

There was the scent of flowers and the fountain was still throwing its water high into the sky.

If it had been iridescent like a rainbow in the sunshine, it looked like silver in the starlight.

It was very lovely and very romantic.

It was the first time in his life that he had ever waved goodnight from the garden to a woman he desired.

He reached the fountain and stood in front of it.

As he had last night, he looked up, waiting for Valeria to appear.

It was then that he heard a scream, and thought he must be mistaken.

Then he heard her scream again and ran faster than he had run for many years back to the Hôtel.

He did not stop to speak to the Porter, but went up the stairs two at a time, thinking it fortunate he knew where her room was.

Actually he was thinking of entering the Sitting-Room.

But he opened the first door he came to and saw in the starlight what was happening.

A man had flung Valeria down on the bed.

He was now trying to lie on top of her as she struggled and screamed.

The *Comte* did not hesitate.

He moved forward and caught hold of the man by the back of his collar.

Lifting him up bodily, he carried him across the room to the balcony.

The man was shouting in Spanish and swearing because the *Comte* had taken him by surprise.

When he realised what was happening, he yelled as loudly as it was possible to do, but it was too late.

The *Comte* flung him over the balcony and he fell onto the lawn beneath it.

It was not very far to the ground, as the rooms in the Hôtel were low-ceilinged.

Although the Spaniard fell heavily, he did not break any of his limbs.

He lay prostrate for a moment, getting back his breath.

Then, swearing and cursing in his own language, he struggled to his feet.

The *Comte* did not wait to see him limp away.

He walked back into the bedroom to where Valeria was sitting up on the bed.

For a moment the *Comte* just stood looking at her in the starlight.

Her eyes were wide with terror and her hair was falling over her shoulders.

Then, as he held out his arms, she rushed towards him.

She clung to him frantically, saying in a voice that was almost incoherent:

"You . . . saved me . . . you saved . . . me! What . . . would have . . . happened . . . if you . . . had . . . not been . . . here?"

The *Comte* held her close.

He could feel her whole body trembling against his.

Valeria was so upset that she had spoken to him in English, and now in the same language he said:

"It all right, my darling. He will not trouble you again, and I will look after and protect you."

Although she was still frantic with the horror of what had happened, Valeria realised he was speaking in English.

She looked up at him in astonishment.

"You can . . . speak . . . English!"

"Of course!" he answered. "And perhaps you understand me more clearly, my precious, when I promise you that this shall never occur again."

She looked at him, trying to understand.

Then, as if he could not help himself, he bent his head and his lips were on hers.

For a moment Valeria stiffened in surprise.

Then, as the lightning moved through her whole body, she melted into the *Comte*'s.

He kissed her gently, as if he were afraid to frighten her more than she was already.

To Valeria he gave her the dreamlike happiness she had known all day.

He also took the stars from the sky and placed them in her arms.

She had never been kissed, and she had no idea she could feel such sensations.

It was an indescribable ecstasy which made it impossible to think, but only to feel.

The *Comte* kissed her until she thought no one could feel such rapture and still be alive.

Then at last he raised his head, and said in a voice that sounded strange and unsteady:

"Now you know what I have been wanting to say to you all day!"

"I . . . I did not know a . . . kiss could . . . be so . . . wonderful!" Valeria answered.

The *Comte* did not answer.

He merely kissed her again a little more demandingly and very possessively.

She could feel the strength of his arms.

She thought that everything in the world had vanished except him.

It was as if centuries had passed, although it was only a few minutes before the *Comte* said:

"I must leave you, my darling, because I know you are tired and upset by what has happened. Tomorrow we will make plans, and there will be no need to go on pretending we do not belong to each other."

"I . . . I love . . . you," Valeria whispered.

"As I love you!" the Comte said. "And I have to look after you, and that I intend to do."

He kissed her very gently.

She thought he was leaving her because it would be a mistake for Tony to return and know what had happened.

"When I have gone," the *Comte* said, "I want you to lock your door, and also the one into the Sitting-Room. While there is no chance of that swine returning, I will tell the Porter that no one except your friend must be allowed in."

"The Spaniard will . . . not come . . . back?" Valeria queried.

Then she gave a little cry.

"You have not . . . killed him?"

"No, of course not," the *Comte* replied, "but he will be bruised and too humiliated to make any attempt to see you again. Anyway, tomorrow I am taking you away from here."

It was then Valeria remembered what was happening tomorrow.

For a moment she shut her eyes at the thought of it.

"You are tired," the *Comte* said gently. "Goodnight, my lovely one! Leave everything to me, and just think of how happy we shall be."

He kissed her forehead.

Then, as if he were forcing himself to be very controlled, he walked to the Sitting-Room and locked the door.

As he reached the door into the passage, he turned round to say:

"Lock this as soon as I have gone, and think of nothing but our love."

He went out, shutting the door quietly.

Because she knew she must obey him, Valeria locked the door knowing he was listening outside to hear her doing so.

She heard his footsteps going down the stairs and listened until there was only silence.

As she moved back towards the bed, tears began to pour down her cheeks.

She tried to wipe them away, but it was impossible to stem the flow.

She flung herself down on the bed to cry into the pillow until she was completely exhausted.

* * *

It was a long time later before Valeria was able to drag herself up, undress, and get back into bed.

She thought it would be impossible to sleep, but she was actually so tired that she was oblivious to everything.

She was aroused only by the sound of someone knocking on her door.

She did not want to wake up.

She turned over with a murmur of complaint at having to come back to consciousness.

It was then she was aware of Tony's voice saying:

"Vala, wake up! Vala!"

She sat up in bed.

She realised that Tony was at the door which led in the Sitting-Room, which was locked.

"Vala!" he called again. "Vala, I want you!"

She got out of bed feeling, because she was so sleepy, unsteady on her feet.

She found the key of the door, opened it, and Tony came into the room.

"I was . . . asleep," she said.

"I know that," Tony answered, "but we have to leave at once."

He walked to the window and pulled back the curtains.

Valeria had drawn them before she had finally got into bed.

Outside, the first fingers of the dawn were creeping up the sky.

There was enough light to show her that Tony was looking somewhat dishevelled.

Although he was wearing his evening-coat, there was white powder on his shoulder and his tie was undone.

"What . . . has . . . happened?" she asked.

"There is no time to explain," Tony said. "We have to leave immediately. Get dressed and pack quickly. There is no time to be lost."

"I . . . I do not . . . understand," Valeria cried.

"I will explain later," Tony said. "Just do as I say, and hurry! I will get my own things."

He left the room almost at a run.

She heard him moving about in his bedroom.

Because she was frightened at what he had said, she dressed hurriedly as he had told her to do.

Fortunately, because she knew they were leaving that morning, she had packed her trunk.

She had put in everything but a day-gown she intended wearing to go back to the yacht.

She placed her blue evening-gown on top of her trunk and pulled on the dress she had left hanging in the wardrobe.

There would be nobody to see her at this time of the morning.

Therefore she merely twisted her long hair into a bun at the back of her head.

The cosmetics she had borrowed from her cousin she pushed into her dressing-case.

She had just finished putting the feathered hat she had worn last night into her hat-box when Tony came back.

"Are you ready?" she asked.

"I . . . think so."

"You can carry your own dressing-case down-stairs," he said. "I will send the Porter up for the rest."

He opened the door onto the landing.

Valeria hurried down the stairs carrying her dressing-case in one hand and the smart hat that went with the gown she was wearing in the other.

It seemed ridiculous to put it on.

Half-way down the stairs she encountered the Porter coming up to collect her trunk.

Through the open front-door she could see a carriage waiting.

She hardly had time to settle herself on the back seat before the luggage had been strapped up behind.

Tony tipped the Porter and joined her.

The horses drove off, and Valeria asked nervously:

"Where are . . . we going . . . what has . . . happened?"

"We are going back to the yacht, of course," Tony replied, "and I think I am safe now, but it has been a near thing!"

"Explain, Tony . . . please . . . explain!" Valeria begged.

Tony looked out of the window at the back of the carriage.

As if relieved to see that nobody was following them, he settled himself more comfortably and put up his feet.

"I suppose you will think I have been a fool!" he began. "At the same time, if we get away unscathed, I can only say it has been worth it!"

"G-get away . . . from what?" Valeria asked.

Tony hesitated. Then he said:

"I suppose I ought not to tell you this, but I feel it would be unfair to leave you in ignorance."

"Of course it would!" Valeria agreed. "And whatever has happened . . . we are in this . . . together."

Tony smiled.

"I always said you were a sport, and that is what you have been."

He gave an unexpected laugh.

"I wanted an adventure, and by God, I have had one!"

"Tell me . . . tell me everything . . . from the very . . . beginning," Valeria pleaded.

Tony drew in his breath.

"You saw I was taken with Renée from the moment I saw her in the *Moulin*."

"Yes . . . of course . . . I realised . . . that," Valeria agreed.

"Well, I spent a marvellous time with her last night."

"At . . . the party?"

"There was no party."

Valeria gave a little gasp.

"Y-you mean . . . you . . . ?"

"Yes, of course that is what I mean!" Tony said as she paused. "And I can tell you, Vala, it was one of the most enjoyable nights I have ever spent!"

Valeria said nothing.

She supposed she ought to be shocked, but she knew that her Grandmother would say "men must be men."

It was what she might have expected.

"Naturally," Tony was saying, "it was easy to see

Renée today, and you said you would be all right with the *Comte,* so we had a very good time and enjoyed ourselves in the afternoon."

"Where . . . did you . . . go?" Valeria asked a little faintly.

"Renée has a small flat—very small—near the *Moulin.* Although it is immaterial, the rent is paid for by the owners of the Dance-Hall."

Valeria was listening, trying to understand.

"Tonight Renée had to go to work as usual, but because I was with her, she could, of course, sit with me, and there was no question of her being taken off by anybody else."

"So you . . . saw the Show . . . again?"

"I did, and Mimi Blanc was absolutely fantastic! I have never seen anything like it!"

Valeria gave a little shudder which he did not notice.

"The whole place got a bit noisy during her performance. Men started throwing things about and the Management had to tell them to behave or they would not see the *Can-Can!*"

"Did you see it?"

"Yes, and it was even better than it was last night."

"I thought you were going to meet the girls after the Show."

"I did," Tony said, "and I stood them all champagne. It made them perform even better, I thought, when they appeared for the second time."

"You watched the second Show as well?" Valeria asked.

"One cannot have too much of a good thing," Tony said as he laughed.

He did not say any more, and after a moment Valeria asked;

"What . . . happened . . . then?"

"I took Renée out to supper, and as you can imagine, by that time it was very late."

He paused as if he were thinking over what had happened, then said:

"I suppose we had both drunk rather a lot, but you know I have always been pretty good at keeping my head. It was only when Renée was hurrying me back to her flat that I sensed something was wrong."

"Something was . . . wrong?" Valeria repeated. "What . . . was it?"

"That is what I was asking myself," Tony replied, "because it seemed strange that Renée was so eager for us to go back when we were comfortable in the Restaurant, and there was plenty to drink."

Valeria waited.

She was trying to understand what had happened.

She still had no idea why, at this hour of the morning, Tony had dragged her away from the Hôtel.

"We were not very far from Renée's flat," he went on after a few minutes. "I thought we could walk there, thinking the night air would sober us up."

"I expect it was a . . . good idea," Valeria said.

"She said she was too tired to walk," Tony went on, "so we found a carriage. We had some difficulty, as there were not many about at that time of the night, and when we reached the flat I told him to wait."

He gave a sigh.

"Thank God I did so! I was really thinking it would be a ghastly bore if I had to walk all the way back to the Hôtel!"

"He waited . . . for you," Valeria prompted.

"He was quite prepared to do so as long as I would pay him what he asked, which, of course, was double the usual fare."

"Then what happened?"

"We went up to Renée's flat, and I suppose that instinct which both you and I have about things must have begun to work, for I suddenly thought it was strange that she was in a hurry."

He paused before he went on:

"I also thought, although I was not certain, that there was a man lurking in the shadows as we went up the stairs, but he moved quickly away when I looked at him."

"A man!" Valeria said. "Who was he?"

"I could not see his face," Tony said. "When we got inside the flat I suggested we should have another drink. I knew she had some wine because I had bought it myself before we went to the *Moulin*."

Valeria thought it was a bad thing to drink so much.

However, she said nothing and he went on:

"Renée refused and pulled me into the bedroom and it was then, quite suddenly, I was suspicious."

"Suspicious . . . of . . . what?" Valeria enquired.

"The man in the shadows," Tony said. "I remembered one of my friends had warned me when we were talking about this sort of thing in London."

"What did he say?"

"He said you always had to be careful that someone you picked up in Dance-Halls and those sorts of places did not attempt to blackmail you by producing a 'husband.' "

Valeria gave a little cry.

"A husband? Do you mean to say she is married?"

"No, of course she is not *really* married, or at any rate, it is unlikely," Tony answered.

"But you said . . ."

"Try to understand, Vala," he said as if he thought his sister was being very stupid. "If a man suddenly appears in the middle of the night when one is in a—compromising situation with the woman he called his 'wife,' there is nothing you can do but pay up!"

Valeria turned her head to stare at him.

"You mean . . . you would have to pay a very large sum of money to prevent him from causing a scandal?"

"Now you understand!" Tony said. "And although there was no likelihood of a scandal, I had no wish to be knocked about until I paid, especially when the moment he was likely to appear, I would not have been looking—as you might say—very dignified!"

Valeria blushed at the thought of how he would have been looking as she said indignantly:

"I think it is the most disgraceful thing I have ever heard!"

"Of course it is," Tony said blithely, "but I managed to get the better of them."

He chuckled as he said:

"I am longing to tell my friends how clever I was!"

"You cannot tell anyone!" Valeria exclaimed in horror. "But . . . what did . . . you . . . do?"

"I was just going to undress," Tony replied, "when I said:

" 'Good Heavens, I have just remembered—I have a present for you! I left it in the carriage!'

" 'What is it?' Renée asked.

" 'It is something which will sparkle as brightly as your eyes!' I replied. 'And I want you to wear it for me.'

"I knew she thought it was a piece of jewellery, so she did not protest when I hurried into my coat and ran down the stairs."

"So you got . . . away!" Valeria said breathlessly.

"I said to the coachman:

" 'Drive like hell and I will pay you double what I have already promised you!' "

Tony chuckled again.

"He must have guessed something was up. He whipped up his horses and they moved a good deal quicker than they had ever done before!"

"So you came to the Hôtel."

"I was rather worried in case the chap passing himself off as Renée's husband would follow me, but first he would have to have found a carriage, and there was no sign of one in the street when I left."

Valeria gave a sigh of relief.

"I think it was very clever of you! At the same time, it is very . . . frightening, and I hope you never have to face such . . . a situation . . . again!"

"If I am, I shall be a good deal more wary than I was this time!" Tony said.

"He might have hurt you . . . and I do not suppose you had very much money on you."

"Those sort of devils will take a cheque, then

132

hold one prisoner until they have cashed it," Tony said, "or else they might have made you give them everything you possessed."

Valeria put up her hands in horror.

"We can only be very grateful that has not happened! Oh, Tony, how could you run such risks? And think how ghastly it would be if Papa ever found out about it!"

"Nobody is going to know about it except you and me," Tony said, "and you are not likely to talk."

"No, of course not, you can be sure of that!" Valeria agreed. "But it seems to me horrible that *Mademoiselle* Renée, who looked such a pleasant girl, should try to trap you in that disgusting manner."

"It will teach me a lesson never to trust anyone!" Tony remarked. "At the same time, I liked Renée and she had a terrific sense of humour."

He was speaking like a small boy who had eaten the whole box of chocolates.

Valeria said with a sigh:

"Well, at least you have seen the *Can-Can*."

"That is what matters more than anything else," Tony agreed, "and I do not mind betting now that we have been through all this trouble to get to the *Moulin,* as soon as we return home Papa will at last decide to give me permission to go to Paris!"

Valeria laughed.

"It is just what might happen! But . . . please . . . please, Tony . . . be very careful not to let anybody know that we have . . . behaved in this . . . outrageous manner. Our relations would be . . . terribly shocked that I had . . . been to the . . . *Moulin de la Mer.*"

"I know that," Tony said, "and I promise you I

will be very careful. I suppose the *Comte* has no idea that we are anything but what we appear to be?"

When he spoke of the *Comte* Valeria felt as if he had plunged a dagger into her breast.

There was silence until she said in a voice that she could not help sounding despondent:

"No, he was not in the least suspicious and . . . of . . . course . . . we shall never . . . see him . . . again!"

chapter seven

VALERIA was woken by the sound of the engines throbbing beneath her.

She realised that the yacht must be moving from the position in the Port where it had not been noticed.

It would go to one of the more fashionable Quays.

It was from there that the *Duc* had arranged to have them collected.

She made a little murmur at being woken, then turned over and went to sleep again.

Last night when they had arrived on board the *Sea Serpent* the Seaman on night watch were astonished to see them.

Valeria left all the explanations to Tony and went below to her cabin.

She pulled off her clothes, put on her nightgown, and got into bed.

As her head touched the pillow she fell asleep.

When she finally awoke again she realised that it was late in the morning and doubtless near to luncheon-time.

She had, however, when they were in the carriage, asked Tony what time they would be collected.

"I told the *Duc* in my letter that we expected to reach St. Jean sometime during the morning of the twentieth," he replied, "and I suggested, politely, that he might like to send a carriage for us at around two o'clock."

Valeria thought that gave her plenty of time to dress.

She also hoped there had been no trouble about their strange arrival at dawn.

When she was ready she went up to the Saloon and found Tony reading a newspaper.

"Good morning, Vala!" he said heartily.

"Is . . . everything . . . all right?" she asked in a low voice.

He smiled.

"I told the Captain there was so much noise at the house where we were staying that we could stand it no longer, so instead of going to bed and trying to sleep, we decided to return to the yacht."

Valeria laughed.

"That was clever! He did not think it strange?"

"Of course not," Tony replied, "why should he? And you know, Vala . . ."

She gave a sudden cry and held up her hand.

"I think it would be a mistake while we are in France for you to call me 'Vala.'"

Tony considered what she had said, then replied:

"I suppose you are thinking that the *Comte* might

know the *Duc* and make a passing reference to a woman known to him as *Madame* Vala Hérard."

Valeria nodded.

"It is always a mistake to leave untidy ends," she said, "and if one is going to lie, then it has to be a really good one."

She made a sound that was almost a sob as she said:

"It is . . . something I hope I . . . never have to . . . do again."

She was thinking as she spoke that she would suffer for the rest of her life for the lies she had been telling.

She would never meet a man she would love in the same way as she loved the *Comte*.

But because it pleased Tony, she had pretended to be a woman of whom her Father and Mother would be ashamed.

He would never know the truth.

" 'One lie leads to another!' "

She could hear her Nanny saying this when she was a child.

Later, because Nanny was fond of preaching to her charges, she used to say:

" 'Sin casts a long shadow!' "

"It is a shadow that will haunt me," Valeria told herself.

She knew, however, it would be a mistake to let Tony know how unhappy she was.

She therefore made a tremendous effort during luncheon to talk amusingly of what had occurred.

She even laughed at the way he had managed to extricate himself from a difficult situation last night.

"I suppose there is . . . nothing they can . . . do now?" she asked a little nervously.

"Nothing!" Tony replied firmly. "And I only hope they are feeling ashamed of themselves."

Valeria saw the expression on his face, and he said:

"All right, I know what you are thinking—they will find another 'greenhorn' like me—but next time I will be more careful!"

When Valeria did not speak, he said:

"Anyway, if Papa has anything to do with it, I do not suppose there will be a 'next time.'"

Valeria knew Tony had had a very lucky escape.

But it would be a great mistake to go on talking about it.

Instead, she discussed the horses they were going to see.

She wondered if the *Duc*'s Château was really as marvellous as her Grandmother had described it.

"If you ask me, these Châteaux all look the same!" Tony complained. "And that goes for their owners!"

"If you are saying that all Frenchmen look alike to you," Valeria retorted, "it is what the Chinese say about us."

"And we say about them," Tony replied, "and actually it is the truth. All Frenchmen are small, dark, and where women are concerned, too busy at 'kissing their hands'!"

Valeria laughed, then she said:

"At least they have beautiful manners, and you had better polish up yours unless you want the *Duc* to send Papa a bad report."

"Report?" Tony exclaimed. "Coming to stay with

your relations will, I am certain, be just like going back to School."

"It will not be for long," Valeria said consolingly. "And I think it would be wise, if they suggest it, if we did not visit Biarritz."

Tony agreed.

She knew that if she returned there she would be searching everywhere for one face belonging to just one man.

'He will soon forget me,' she told herself, and almost cried at the pain of it.

A carriage arrived at the Quay at exactly two o'clock.

It was a very comfortable vehicle drawn by four perfectly matched horses.

They were one of the finest teams that Valeria had ever seen.

She patted them and complimented the coachman, which obviously pleased him.

As it was such a warm day, the hood of the carriage was open.

As they drove off, Valeria looked with joy at the surrounding countryside.

When a little later they had a fine view of the Pyrenees, she pointed them out to Tony almost triumphantly.

"I told you it was a part of France that was very beautiful," she said, "and in contrast, I feel now that Normandy is too flat!"

Tony, however, was not really listening.

After a time they drove in silence, and Valeria kept the beauty she was seeing to herself.

Although the horses went very fast, it took them

over two hours to reach the Château.

When they saw it, Valeria knew that her Grandmother had not exaggerated.

It was undoubtedly the most beautiful place she had ever seen.

It was also magnificent.

Built in the reign of Louis XIV, it was in a part of France that did not suffer greatly from the Revolution.

The cupolas and towers made the Château seem from a distance to look like a Fairy Palace.

When they drove nearer, Valeria had her first glimpse of the exquisitely laid out gardens.

There were two fountains playing in the front of the Château and three in the gardens behind.

From the moment she entered the house itself Valeria knew it was the most beautiful place she had ever imagined.

She was to find later that every room was more breathtaking than the last.

They were greeted by the *Duc*'s Grandmother, who, Valeria thought, was very like her own *grandmère*.

She had the same elegance, the same mellow beauty of old age.

Also the same irresistible French charm.

It was typical, Valeria thought, of their politeness that because Tony was English, everybody talked in his language rather than their own.

Even the small children that belonged to several cousins who were present managed to be quite fluent.

From the way the family looked at her, and also from the compliments they paid her, Valeria was aware from the moment she arrived what they were thinking.

The *Duc*'s relations were well aware why her Grandmother was so eager for her to be a guest at the Château.

There was, however, no sign of the *Duc*.

It would have been impolite to ask the cause of his absence, so nothing was said.

At seven o'clock it was time to go upstairs and dress for dinner.

Before this, Valeria had seen the main State-Rooms in the Château.

She was thinking of their architectural perfection as well as the beautiful way in which they were decorated.

The whole Château was undoubtedly unique.

The *Duc*'s Grandmother was delighted that everything pleased Valeria so much.

As they went upstairs she said to her:

"I know Claudius will be pleased that you admire his house. He is very proud of it, as we all are, and as you can guess, my dear, we are all longing for him to have a son to inherit it."

"I am sure there is . . . plenty of time for . . . that," Valeria said evasively.

The *Duchesse* sighed.

"Whoever knows what might happen in the future? There could be another war, a Revolution, or perhaps an accident."

Valeria did not know what to say, and she went on:

"It is all, of course, in the hands of *Le Bon Dieu,* and I can only pray that Claudius will forget how deeply he was hurt in the past."

141

Valeria knew that the *Duchesse* was referring to the *Duc*'s insane wife.

She was sorry for him and his family, but she told herself it was none of her business.

It was a problem they must solve for themselves.

She had been allotted one of the beautiful State-Rooms on the First Floor which overlooked the garden.

When the *Duchesse* left her, she went to the window, where she could see a fountain playing.

It brought back vividly the memory of the *Comte* standing waiting for her to wave to him.

The fountain that was playing now was enormous.

The water rose above the head of an exquisitely carved statue of Venus surrounded by small Cupids.

The stone basin was also decorated with Cupids, and the whole sculpture was exceedingly beautiful.

But Valeria could see only the small fountain behind the *Comte*.

She knew that wherever he was at this moment her heart went out to him.

She would never see a fountain again without feeling it tore her heart in pieces.

She turned from the window feeling she could not bear to look at it any more.

The maid was already laying out her clothes.

Tonight she would wear the white gown of a *débutante,* with no jewellery.

There would be only a white rose at the side of her head.

It was, in fact, a very lovely gown.

It had been bought for her to wear at one of the most important Balls of the Season.

She would have been foolish if she had not realised that she stood out amongst all the other girls that were present.

It was not only her beauty which detracted from them, but the fact that she was so elegantly gowned.

When she was ready, Tony came into the room to take her downstairs.

She had asked him to do so thinking she might feel shy on her first night.

She also thought it would give her courage when she had to meet the "Awesome *Duc*."

She supposed he would turn up in time for dinner.

He had not been there to greet them earlier in the afternoon.

As Tony joined her, the maid tactfully left the room.

"What do you think of the party?" Valeria asked.

"I am glad to find there are at least two pretty girls," Tony replied, "and there are several men of my own age with whom I shall enjoy riding."

"Try to enjoy yourself," Valeria said, "and you must admit, the Château is magnificent!"

"It is certainly smarter than the *Moulin de la Mer*!" Tony remarked provocatively.

Valeria gave a cry and put her fingers to her lips.

"For Heaven's sake, Tony, do be careful!" she warned. "I have never heard of the place!"

"I will be very careful," Tony promised. "Now, come along, I am hungry and one thing I will say for the French is that they do produce good food."

They went together down the magnificent gilt and crystal staircase.

A footman opened the door of the Salon, where they had been told everybody would be assembled before dinner.

There must have been about twenty people already gathered, but there was still no sign of the *Duc*.

It suddenly struck Valeria that perhaps he was reluctant to be bored by his English visitors, 'in which case,' she thought, 'we will be able to leave earlier than we intended.'

The older members of the party were sipping champagne.

Valeria realised with amusement that she was not offered a glass.

Then she was aware that the *Duchesse* was glancing at the clock as if she thought dinner was late.

As she did so, the door opened and a man came in.

"Claudius!" the *Duchesse* exclaimed. "I was wondering what had happened to you!"

"Forgive me, Grandmama."

As he spoke, Valeria turned round and felt as if she were frozen to the floor.

It was not the *Duc* who was bending politely over the hand of his Grandmother, but the *Comte*.

For a moment Valeria thought she must be seeing a mirage and her eyes were deceiving her.

But how could she not recognise him?

His dark hair brushed back from his square forehead, his eyes, which so often made her feel shy!

"You are very naughty to be so late!" the *Duchesse*

was saying. "Our guests have arrived from England and are looking forward to meeting you. Let me introduce to you the Viscount Strang, who has taken his father's place, because, as you know, the Earl has had a bad fall."

The *Duc* held out his hand.

"I am delighted to see you," he said, "and only sorry your Father could not come to visit me as planned."

"My Father is extremely disappointed at not being able to see your horses," Tony said. "I am a poor substitute, but I assure you I am looking forward to admiring them."

It was a pretty speech which Valeria thought Tony must have rehearsed before he came downstairs.

She realised as he was speaking that he had not recognised the *Duc* as being the *Comte* de Savin.

When she thought about it, it was not really surprising.

Tony had seen him only once in the dim light of the *Moulin de la Mer*.

At that moment he had been interested in nothing but the *Can-Can* he had waited for so long to see.

"And now," the *Duchesse* was saying, "you must meet your cousin Lady Valeria Netherton, who has, I am told, been the *'Belle'* of every Ball this Season in London."

Valeria still could not move.

She also could not raise her eyes to meet the *Duc*'s.

Then she heard him say in his deep voice:

"I am delighted to meet you, Lady Valeria, and

to welcome you to my Château."

He spoke in English in a calm, cold manner, which struck her as surprising.

She looked up at him.

As she did so, he turned away to speak to one of his relatives.

It seemed incredible, but he had not recognised her!

Then she told herself that she now looked very different from the rouged, mascaraed, and powdered *"Madame* Hérard."

Dinner was announced, and the *Duc* escorted one of his guests, who was a *Marquise,* in to dinner.

She sat on his right, and as there were more men than women, Tony, as a newcomer, sat on his left.

Valeria had two young men who were distant relatives on each side of her.

They paid her extravagant compliments.

They managed to keep her and themselves laughing all through the meal.

She had, however, no idea what she ate and little idea of what she said.

Every nerve in her body was tinglingly aware of the *Duc.*

He was sitting at the head of the table looking magnificent, and at the same time very aloof.

He was, in fact, exactly what she had expected him to be.

Very grand, puffed up with his own consequence, and of the opinion that most people were beneath his condescension.

If this was the *Duc* de Laparde, what she wanted was *Comte* Ramon de Savin.

Ramon, who had kissed her and given her sensations she had not known existed.

Ramon, who had stolen her heart.

She had thought it would never beat again, until he had come into the Salon, not as himself, but as the *Duc*.

'He does not recognise me,' she kept thinking, 'and if he did, no doubt he would be horrified at the way I have behaved.'

She thought it would be impossible to go through a whole week of being near him.

How could she hear him speak without betraying herself?

In fact, she thought, the only thing to do was to make some excuse to return to England as quickly as possible.

It would not be easy.

She knew her decision would be questioned not only by the *Duc*'s family, but also by Tony.

'What can I do? What can I do?' she was asking herself as the young men beside her teased her.

They also made wittily disparaging remarks about the English, whom they expected her to defend.

At last dinner came to an end.

As was usual in France, the gentlemen did not stop to drink their port alone as they did in England.

They left the *Salle à Manager* with the ladies.

They all moved into a different Salon from the one they had been in before dinner.

Out of this room, which was very elegant and beautiful, there was a Card-Room.

The younger members of the party repaired to it immediately on the *Duc*'s direction.

There was a large brilliantly lit billiard-table.

Valeria heard one of the men challenging Tony, who agreed with alacrity to a game.

There were all sort of other games.

There were Bridge tables for the older guests, Darts, Backgammon, and even a miniature Skittles Alley.

The *Duc* was placing everybody where he thought they would enjoy themselves most.

Valeria, watching him, wondered what she would be told to do.

Unexpectedly the *Duc* said to her:

"I have something to show you, Lady Valeria, which I think you will find interesting."

He spoke in the same cold, austere manner in which he had spoken when he arrived.

She followed him back into the Salon and out through a door which led into a corridor.

It was decorated with furniture which would have graced any Museum.

There were portraits of the Laparde family which had been painted by the great Masters of the time.

Valeria, however, could think of nothing but the fact that Ramon was beside her.

She wanted to put out her hand to touch him, to make certain he was really there.

He opened a door.

They went into a very attractive room which she had not been shown before.

The furniture was more comfortable than classic, and there was a writing-desk.

She thought perhaps it was the one the *Duc* used himself.

They walked across the room to where there were four pictures on the wall.

"I think this is what you wanted to see!" he said.

She looked up at them.

For the moment she did not understand why he had brought her to see them.

Then she realised they were Impressionists.

There was no mistaking the manner in which they were painted—the brilliant colours, the strange light, and the lack of darkness to which every Impressionist subscribed.

"These two," the *Duc* said pointing, "are by Monet. This one is by Sisley, and this by Degas. And you said, '*Madame* Hérard,' that was what you wanted to see!"

Valeria gave a little gasp.

"Y-you . . . knew who I was!"

"I am not blind!" the *Duc* said curtly.

There was silence. Then Valeria asked:

"Are you . . . very . . . shocked?"

"It is not a question of being shocked," the *Duc* said, "but I am angry, very angry indeed at the way you left without telling me!"

Valeria drew in her breath.

Now there was a condemnation in his voice she could not ignore.

"I . . . I am sorry . . . terribly sorry," she said, "but . . . Tony was . . . in trouble . . . and we . . . had to . . . leave!"

"In the middle of the night, I understand."

"H-how do you . . . know . . . that?"

"When I called to collect you from the Hôtel this afternoon at twelve-thirty," the *Duc* said, "I could

149

hardly believe you had gone without leaving me a message and you had just disappeared in that extraordinary manner."

"It was . . . what we had . . . to do . . . anyway," Valeria said unhappily.

"Why?"

"Because . . . Tony had . . . stolen two . . . extra days of the . . . visit . . . so that he . . . could . . . see the *Can-Can* at . . . the *Moulin de la Mer*."

"That is one thing," the *Duc* said, "but I thought what you and I felt for each other was something— different."

"I . . . know," Valeria replied, "but h-how could I . . . have g-guessed that . . . you would be . . . pretending to be . . . someone you . . . were not . . . just as . . . I was?"

"Ramon is one of the names with which I was christened," the *Duc* replied, "just as 'de Savin' is one of my titles."

Valeria could not look at him.

She only said in a low voice:

"If I had . . . not pretended . . . to be . . . a widow . . . I could not have . . . accompanied Tony . . . to the *Moulin* and would . . . have to have . . . stayed behind . . . alone in the Hôtel."

"I realise that," the *Duc* said. "At the same time, dressed as you were, you might have expected to run into a great deal of danger."

"Of course I did not . . . expect that!" Valeria said. "How could I have . . . thought that any . . . man would behave as the Spaniard did? But . . . you saved me!"

"I might not have been there," the *Duc* said, "in

which case, God knows what might have happened to you!"

He spoke so severely that Valeria gave a little cry and said:

"You will not . . . tell Papa . . . oh, promise me . . . you will not tell Papa!"

There was silence, and she said again:

"Please . . . promise! He would be furious if he knew . . . both with Tony and . . . with me."

"If I promise," the *Duc* said slowly, "what do you intend to do about us?"

Valeria made a helpless little gesture with her hand.

"T-Tony did not recognise you tonight. After all, he has seen you only once . . . and when we have gone back to England . . . you can . . . forget about m-me."

She thought as she spoke that was what would happen, but she would never be able to forget him.

They were still standing in front of the Impressionist pictures, but the *Duc* was looking at her.

She dare not meet his eyes, and she waited, praying that he would keep his word and not tell her Father how badly she and Tony had behaved.

"I am waiting for an answer to my question," the *Duc* said.

"I have . . . told you . . . what must . . . happen."

"And what is Ramon de Savin," he enquired, "to do about *Madame* Hérard?"

Valeria made a gesture that was very French.

Strangely enough, they were talking in English, as they had done during dinner.

Unexpectedly the *Duc* said in a very different voice:

"What did you feel after I left you last night and you knew you would never see me again?"

Valeria remembered how she had cried despairingly at the agony it had been.

"There . . . there was . . . nothing I could . . . do," she whispered.

"I said I would look after you and protect you," the *Duc* said, "and that is what I meant to do."

"In a *garçonnière* in . . . Paris?" Valeria flashed. "You know . . . now that is . . . impossible."

"I knew it before," the *Duc* said, "but you bemused and bewildered me, although I was quite certain you were not who you pretended to be."

"H-how . . . did you find . . . out who . . . I was?" Valeria asked.

"It drove me nearly mad when I learnt you had left the Hôtel," the *Duc* said, "leaving no forwarding address and without, as I might have expected, a note for me!"

Once again he was speaking as if what he had suffered had made him angry.

"I questioned every Porter in the Hôtel," he went on, "but they could tell me nothing until somebody suggested that the Night Porter might be able to help."

Valeria remembered that it was the Night Porter to whom Tony had paid the bill.

He had also carried down her luggage.

"He told you . . . where we . . . had gone?" she asked.

"When he came on duty at four o'clock," the *Duc* replied, "he told me how you had driven away in a hectic fashion, but he did not know where. He did, however, give me the name of the driver of the carriage you had hired."

"He told ... you that ... he took us ... to the Quay?"

"To a yacht called the *Sea Serpent*," the *Duc* replied.

"A-and ... were you ... surprised?"

"I was shocked—appalled and, if you like, very angry that a *jeune fille* should have been to the *Moulin* and had also been assaulted by a Spaniard, although it was what she deserved!"

There was silence before Valeria said:

"I understand ... what you ... feel and ... therefore as I was ... thinking at dinner ... the sooner ... Tony and I ... go back to England ... the better!"

It was difficult to say the words without crying.

With a superhuman effort she kept the tears from coming into her eyes.

"Do you really think I would let you do that?" the *Duc* asked.

His arms went round her, and he was pulling her against him.

For a moment Valeria could hardly believe it was happening.

Then the *Duc*'s lips were on hers, he was kissing her, and the whole world turned a somersault.

He kissed her gently and possessively as he had done before.

Then, as she felt an ecstasy rise within her, he lifted his head to say very quietly:

"How soon will you marry me, my darling?"

She stared at him.

Her face was radiant, as if a thousand candles had been lit inside her.

He thought it was impossible for any woman to look so beautiful.

At the same time, she was unearthly and unhuman.

Then she said, and her voice seemed unexpectedly strong:

"No!"

The *Duc* stared at her.

Because his arms had slackened, she moved away from him.

She walked blindly across the room to stand at the window.

The sun was just sinking, turning the water spewed up by the fountain to crimson.

The *Duc* looked at her silhouetted against the window before he asked:

"Are you really refusing to marry me?"

There was a note of astonishment in his voice.

Having been begged, bullied, and beseeched by his relatives to marry, it had never struck him that any woman would refuse him.

"I thought you loved me."

"I . . . I do love . . . you," Valeria replied, "but . . . I cannot marry you!"

"Why not? You must have a reason!"

"Of . . . course I . . . have a . . . reason."

He walked across the room to stand a little nearer to her.

"I am waiting to hear it."

"It is . . . quite . . . simple," Valeria said. "I love . . . you so . . . much that it . . . will be . . . agony to . . . live without you . . . but if we . . . were married . . . then I . . . lost you . . . I would only . . . want . . . to d-die."

"Why are you so certain that you will lose me?" the *Duc* asked.

"Grandmama has told me of the many . . . women you have . . . loved . . . and who . . . sooner or later you . . . found a . . . bore. They were . . . beautiful, witty, and, being French, intelligent! Why should I . . . prove to be . . . different . . . in any way?"

"So that is the reason why you are saying you will not marry me!" the *Duc* said.

"It is the . . . reason why I . . . dare not marry you!" Valeria answered.

She thought as she spoke that she was deliberately crucifying herself.

Yet now that she knew who Ramon was, she knew it would be impossible for them to be really happy together.

The *Duc* came a little nearer still.

"I suppose your Grandmother, who was always a very talkative woman," he said, "has told you about my marriage?"

"Y-yes . . . and I am very . . . sorry for . . . you."

"I do not want your pity," he said harshly, "but perhaps you can understand why I not only wanted to forget, but also to enjoy myself."

"Of course . . . and being French . . ."

Valeria did not finish the sentence.

"And being French that meant there would be women in my life," the *Duc* said. "As you said, they were beautiful women, witty, amusing, clever!"

Valeria drew in her breath, but she did not speak and he went on:

"But you asked me why they bored me. I could not have told you the reason—until I met you."

Valeria felt a little tremor go through her, but she did not move and he went on:

"Always I was disappointed, but still optimistic. I tried again and again to find that someone who was the other part of myself. They did not necessarily have to be beautiful or witty or amusing. It was just that I wanted someone different, but it was something I could not put into words."

He paused before he continued:

"Then I saw you in the *Moulin* and I felt something go 'click' within me which told me you were exceptional. I cannot explain it—there are no words with which to define it. But the feeling was there, which was why I sat down next to you."

"You . . . really felt I was . . . different?" Valeria asked.

"I knew I had to go on seeing you, I had to be with you. Then after we had dinner and I took you back to your Hôtel I knew that I wanted you not only because you were so beautiful, but because I wanted to talk to you and I wanted to be with you."

His voice deepened as he said:

"The next morning I thought I must have exaggerated my feelings. Then, as you know, we had that dreamlike day together and I knew I had fallen in love completely and irretrievably, and that whatever you were, whatever you had done, I had to keep you with me."

Valeria made a little murmur, and he added:

"It was something I wanted to tell you in the carriage, but you would not let me."

"I thought . . . it might . . . spoil what had been such a . . . wonderful day."

"When I heard you scream," the *Duc* said, "and after I threw that scum out of the window, I knew I could never lose you."

"But you did . . . not intend . . . to marry '*Madame* Hérard'!" Valeria said.

"I did not face that question," the *Duc* answered. "All I knew was that I intended to hold on to her and never let her go and forget she had ever been assaulted by any other man."

"But you . . . still would not . . . have married . . . me!" Valeria persisted.

"If I am to be entirely honest," the *Duc* replied, "I knew that *Madame* Hérard was not a married woman."

"H-how did you know that?" Valeria enquired. "I was . . . wearing a wedding-ring."

The *Duc* smiled.

"You were so absurdly innocent! And if *Madame* Hérard had been as you intended, she would not have shut her eyes while Mimi Blanc was dancing."

"You . . . knew I . . . did that?"

"I was watching you. She would also have flirted with me, which was something you never did!"

He smiled before he said:

"I have never before been with a woman who did not flirt with me, try to entice me, and touch me. Oh, my precious, you are so innocent, so unspoilt, that I am prepared to swear on the Bible that you had never been kissed before I kissed you."

Valeria did not answer, and he said:

"That is true—is it not?"

"It is . . . true but because as you say, I am . . . innocent how could . . . I possibly . . . keep a man

157

who is known as a . . . modern Casanova . . . in love
with . . . me?"

The *Duc* laughed, and it was a very tender sound.

"You will not have to keep me in love with you,"
he said, "but I will always be afraid of losing your
love. You are so beautiful that I am quite certain
it will take me all my time to keep men from pur-
suing you. But I warn you, I will kill any man who
touches you—just as I will kill you if you try to
leave me!"

"But . . . I am trying . . . to tell you that . . . I cannot . . . stay with you," Valeria said in a very small
voice. "Have you thought . . . when I am not . . .
so pretty as . . . I am now . . . or perhaps when I
am . . . having a baby . . . you will find other wom-
en . . . very much more . . . attractive?"

"The Ancient Greeks maintained that there was
nothing more beautiful than a woman with child!"
the *Duc* argued.

"But you are not Greek!"

"No, I am French," he said, "and I can imagine
nothing more wonderful than to know you were
carrying my child and nothing more thrilling than
to see my son in your arms."

"Suppose . . . it was . . . a daughter?" Valeria
asked almost childishly.

The *Duc* smiled.

"In which case, my precious one, we should have
to try again!"

With a swift movement he suddenly turned her
round to face him.

"We cannot go on arguing about it all night," he
said, "but on the fiftieth Anniversary of our marriage you will apologise to me because you were

wrong. I love you and I am going to marry you!"

He did not wait for an answer, but kissed her.

Now his kisses were different from what they had been before.

He kissed her fiercely, demandingly, almost brutally.

He kissed her lips, her neck, the little valley between her breasts, and again her lips.

Valeria knew he was wooing her with kisses, and something wild and ecstatic rose within her to meet the challenge.

She surrendered herself completely, not willingly, but because she could not help it.

He kissed her until they were no longer on the ground but were flying in the sky.

They were touching the stars as they had done the previous night.

Now, however, it was even more rapturous and more wonderful than it had ever been.

The *Duc* kissed Valeria until she felt she must die.

He had taken her to a Heaven where there was only happiness and no problems.

They were enveloped with the blazing, dazzling light of love.

Only when she felt as if the light that was moving within her breast was almost too agonising to be borne did the *Duc* say:

"Now tell me when you will marry me."

"Now . . . at once!" Valeria whispered. "And if . . . I have only a . . . few months of . . . happiness with . . . you it will be . . . better than . . . years of . . . misery without . . . you!"

"We shall be ecstatically happy for ever!" the *Duc* said.

Then he was kissing her again.

* * *

A long time later Valeria found herself sitting on the sofa with her head on the *Duc*'s shoulder.

"I love and adore you," he said, "and now we have to decide how soon we tell my family that you are to be my wife. They will want to jump over the moon when they learn of it!"

"Oh, please," Valeria pleaded, "we cannot do it too hastily, or they will think it strange when you were supposed to have met me for the first time only today!"

"I have known you in a thousand lives before this one," the *Duc* said, "and I will go on loving you for thousands more. Although we were born apart, we can never really be separated from each other."

"Are you . . . quite sure . . . of that?" Valeria asked. "I . . . want to . . . belong to you and . . . I love you! Oh, Ramon . . . how much I love . . . you!"

"As I love you," the *Duc* said, "and if you had not agreed to marry me, I think I would have thrown you into one of the dungeons and beaten you into submission!"

She laughed.

"You said you . . . wanted a . . . challenge . . . and as you have won . . . everything else . . . this is just another . . . trophy."

"The only trophy that matters!" the *Duc* said. "How, my darling, can I have been so fortunate as to find you when I had begun to think in despair that you did not even exist?"

"There I was . . . waiting for . . . you in . . . the *Moulin de la Mer*!" Valeria said provocatively.

"It will always be to me the Windmill of Love," the *Duc* answered. "The wind of love blew me to the *Moulin* and the same wind blew you. Now we are joined together irrevocably by love."

"Oh, Ramon!" Valeria's voice was very moving.

"But let me make it very clear," the *Duc* went on, "that as my *Duchesse* you will behave in a circumspect manner. There will be no more visits to the *Moulin* or any place like it. And if I see you wearing mascara on your already long eye-lashes and rouge on your most kissable lips, I shall be very angry!"

He kissed her again before she could protest.

When at last he set her free she rested her head against him to say:

"I can always . . . threaten you . . . if you are . . . unkind to me or . . . look bored with becoming . . . '*Madame* Hérard' . . . again!"

The *Duc*'s arms tightened.

"She was very desirable in her own way," he admitted, "but the lovely *débutante* I now hold in my arms is quite different!"

"In . . . what . . . way?" Valeria asked because she wanted to hear him saying it.

"Because she is young, innocent, unspoilt, and particularly, although she has not yet said so, because she loves me so much she will do everything I want her to do."

"I have the feeling this is the beginning of an argument which will go on for the rest of our lives!" Valeria said.

"I intend to enthral and enslave you, my darling," the *Duc* said, "and that, although you may not admit it, that is what you really want!"

"Of course it is!" Valeria replied. "And, oh, Ramon, I do love you . . . I love you! I love you . . . with my whole . . . heart and my . . . whole soul!"

"They are all mine!" the *Duc* said.

Then he was kissing her, kissing her until once again they were floating among the stars.

The Light of Love was burning brightly within them.

It enveloped them with a glory from which there was no escape.

They were imprisoned in a windmill of love from now until Eternity.

ABOUT THE AUTHOR

Barbara Cartland, the world's most famous romantic novelist, who is also an historian, playwright, lecturer, political speaker and television personality, has now written over 550 books and sold over 600 million copies all over the world.

She has also had many historical works published and has written four autobiographies as well as the biographies of her mother and that of her brother, Ronald Cartland, who was the first Member of Parliament to be killed in the last war. This book has a preface by Sir Winston Churchill and has just been republished with an introduction by Sir Arthur Bryant.

Love at the Helm, a novel written with the help and inspiration of the late Earl Mountbatten of Burma, Great Uncle of His Royal Highness The Prince of Wales, is being sold for the Mountbatten Memorial Trust.

She has broken the world record for the last sixteen years by writing an average of twenty-three books a year. In the *Guinness Book of Records* she is listed as the world's top-selling author.

Miss Cartland in 1978 sang an Album of Love Songs with the Royal Philharmonic Orchestra.

In private life Barbara Cartland, who is a Dame of the Order of St. John of Jerusalem, Chairman of the St. John Council in Hertfordshire and Deputy President of the St. John Ambulance Brigade, has fought for better conditions and salaries for Midwives and Nurses.

She championed the cause for the Elderly in 1956 invoking a Government Enquiry into the "Housing Conditions of Old People."

In 1962 she had the Law of England changed so that Local Authorities had to provide camps for their own Gypsies. This has meant that since then thousands and thousands of Gypsy children have been able to go to School, which they had never been able to do in the past, as their caravans were moved every twenty-four hours by the Police.

There are now fourteen camps in Hertfordshire and Barbara Cartland has her own Romany Gypsy Camp called Barbaraville by the Gypsies.

Her designs "Decorating with Love" are being sold all over the U.S.A. and the National Home Fashions League made her, in 1981, "Woman of Achievement."

She is unique in that she was one and two in the Dalton list of Best Sellers, and one week had four books in the top twenty.

Barbara Cartland's book *Getting Older, Growing Younger* has been published in Great Britain and the U.S.A. and her fifth cookery book, *The Romance of Food*, is now being used by the House of Commons.

In 1984 she received at Kennedy Airport America's Bishop Wright Air Industry Award for her contribution to the development of aviation. In 1931 she and two R.A.F. Officers thought of, and carried, the first aeroplane-towed glider airmail.

During the war she was Chief Lady Welfare Officer in Bedfordshire looking after 20,000 Service men and women. She thought of having a pool of Wedding Dresses at the War Office so a Service Bride could hire a gown for the day.

She bought 1,000 gowns without coupons for the A.T.S., the W.A.A.F.'s and the W.R.E.N.S. In 1945 Barbara Cartland received the Certificate of Merit from Eastern Command.

In 1964 Barbara Cartland founded the National Association for Health of which she is the President, as a front for all the Health Stores and for any product made as alternative medicine.

This is now a £65 million turnover a year, with one-third going in export.

In January 1988 she received *La Médaille de Vermeil de la Ville de Paris*. This is the highest award to be given in France by the City of Paris. She has sold 25 million books in France.

In March 1988 Barbara Cartland was asked by the Indian Government to open their Health Resort outside Delhi. This is almost the largest Health Resort in the world.

Barbara Cartland was received with great enthusiasm by her fans, who fêted her at a reception in the City, and she received the gift of an embossed plate from the Government.

Barbara Cartland was made a Dame of the Order of the British Empire in the 1991 New Year's Honours List by Her Majesty, The Queen, for her contribution to Literature and also for her years of work for the community.